THE GODDESS AND THE GAIETY GIRL

Barbara Cartland, the world's most famous romantic novelist, who is also an historian, playwright, lecturer, political speaker and television personality, has now written over 280 books.

She has also had many historical works published and has written four autobiographies as well as the biographies of her mother and that of her brother, Ronald Cartland, who was the first Member of Parliament to be killed in the last war. This book has a preface by Sir Winston Churchill.

She has recently completed a very unusual book called *Barbara Cartland's Book of Useless Information*, with a foreword by the Admiral of the Fleet, the late Earl Mountbatten of Burma. This is being sold for the United World Colleges of which he was President.

She has also sung an Album of Love Songs with the Royal Philharmonic Orchestra.

In 1976, by writing twenty-one books, she broke the world record and has continued for the following three years with 24, 20 and 23.

In private life Barbara Cartland, who is a Dame of the Order of St. John of Jerusalem, Chairman of the St. John Council in Hertfordshire and Deputy President of the St. John Ambulance Brigade, has also fought for better conditions and salaries for Midwives and Nurses.

As President of the Royal College of Midwives (Hertfordshire Branch) she has been invested with the first Badge of Office ever given in Great Britain, which was subscribed to by the Midwives themselves. She has also championed the cause for old people, had the law altered regarding gypsies and founded the first Romany Gypsy camp in the world.

Barbara Cartland is deeply interested in Vitamin Therapy and is President of the British National Association for Health. She has a Health and Happiness Club in England and has just started one in America. He

over one million copies t
lated into many languages.

She has a magazine *Barb*
now being published in the

By the same author in Pan Books

For other titles by Barbara Cartland
please see page 157

BARBARA CARTLAND

THE GODDESS
AND THE
GAIETY GIRL

Pan Original
Pan Books London and Sydney

First published 1980 by Pan Books Ltd,
Cavaye Place, London SW10 9PG
© Cartland Promotions 1980
ISBN 0 330 26243 2
Typeset, printed and bound in Great Britain by
Hazell Watson & Viney Ltd, Aylesbury, Bucks

Author's Note

The facts in this novel about Joseph Lister and his discovery of antiseptics are correct, as are references to the Gaiety Theatre.

Arthur, the legendary British King of the Knights of the Round Table, has been a bone of contention among scholars for centuries. But the 9th century *Historia Briton-urn* describes his twelve battles against the Saxons and the *Annales Cambriae, c.* 950–1000, records the battle of Cambran "in which Arthur and Medrant fell".

Alfred Tennyson immortalised Arthur in verse and I like to believe the French legends widely circularised in the 12th century that Arthur never died but is waiting to return to save those who need him, when the world is overcome by evil.

Perhaps that moment is not far away, when good will finally be victorious.

Chapter One
1870

The 4th Duke of Tregaron, Murdoch Proteus Edmond Garon, was dying.

The huge Castle was quiet, the servants moved about on tip-toe, and everywhere there was that tell-tale hush which is the prelude to death.

" 'E be a long time 'bout it," one footman said to another as they waited in the great Gothic hall for the carriages which kept arriving.

"It be them doctors," the flunkey replied. "If ye be poor they polishes ye off quick; if ye be rich they keep ye breathing as long as they can get their fat fees."

The first footman stifled a laugh, then lapsed into silence as the Butler, grey-haired and pontifical, came walking towards the front door.

He must have seen a carriage coming down the long drive bordered by ancient oak trees.

Two footmen hurried down the stone steps to the carriage door and their place was taken by two others, all wearing the claret and gold livery of the Garons, and powdered wigs.

Waiting at the front door, the Butler watched the Dowager Marchioness of Humber step out of the carriage.

He was thinking that it was not surprising that the Duke, after the dissolute and debauched life he had lived, should die at the comparatively early age of fifty-eight.

The Dowager walked slowly and with dignity, because she was a very regal woman, up the steps and into the hall.

"Good-afternoon, Dawson!"

"Good-afternoon, M'Lady," the Butler replied with a bow. "It's a sad day for us all as Your Ladyship knows."

"I will go to His Grace immediately," the Dowager replied. "There is no need for you to accompany me, Dawson. I presume Mr. Justin has been sent for?"

"Yes, M'Lady. I understand a Courier left for France yesterday morning."

"France!"

It was not a question but an exclamation and the Dowager Marchioness pursed her lips in a disapproving manner as she slowly climbed the Grand Staircase with its rich carving of stone work interspersed with heraldic beasts each holding a shield.

Upstairs in the huge bedroom which had once been the sleeping chamber of Kings, the 4th Duke lay with closed eyes and paying no attention to the husky voice of his private Chaplain praying beside him.

On the opposite side of the bed the Duke's sister Lady Alice Garon who was unmarried, sat on a chair.

She was unable to go down on her knees because of her arthritis, and anyway she thought somewhat cynically, neither her brother nor God were likely to appreciate the gesture.

Three doctors stood somewhat awkwardly at the far end of the room talking amongst themselves in whispers.

They had done their best to prolong the life of their patient, but they had known when he developed pneumonia that nothing, and certainly not their somewhat limited skills, would be able to save him.

The door opened and the Dowager Marchioness came in, moving like a ship in full sail.

She walked to her brother's bedside and the Chaplain rose at her approach to melt quietly into the shadows.

The Dowager bent over the bed and laid her hand on her brother's.

"Can you hear me, Murdoch?" she enquired.

The Duke very slowly opened his eyes.

"I am here," the Dowager said, "and I am glad you are still alive!"

A faintly mocking smile twisted the Duke's thin lips.

"You – always wanted – to be – in at the – kill – Muriel!"

The Dowager Marchioness stiffened almost as if she resented the accusation.

Then before she could reply the Duke said in a voice which sounded as if he was gasping for breath:

"Where – is – Justin?"

"I understand they sent for him yesterday," the Dowager answered. "I think it is extremely remiss that it was not done sooner."

She looked directly at her sister on the other side of the bed as she spoke and it was obvious that Lady Alice would have retorted if the Duke had not continued still between exhausted gasps:

"He will – make a better – Duke than – I have."

The last word was lost in a frightening rattle that seemed to come from the base of his throat.

The doctors moved quickly forward but as they reached the bed they knew that the 4th Duke would not speak again...

* * *

The sunshine was trying to percolate through the lace curtains which covered a window that needed cleaning.

As if the warmth of it disturbed the man sitting in an armchair with his feet outstretched, he looked towards the woman lying on a low couch which could be converted into a sofa, to ask:

"It's a warm day. Would you like some air?"

"I don't mind," the woman replied. "If you want to go out, you go."

"I'm all right," the man answered.

"It's ghastly for you being cooped up in here. I know that, but, Harry, I'm so grateful."

She put out her hand as she spoke and the man rose to sit down on the side of the couch holding her hand in his.

"You know I want to be with you, Katie," he said, "and I only wish to God there was something I could do."

The woman who was little more than a girl, sighed.

"So do I, and at this time of the afternoon it's agony not to be going down to the Theatre. I keep thinking of them sitting in the new dressing-room and putting on their pretty clothes. Oh, Harry, who's wearing mine?"

It was a cry that seemed to come from her heart and Harry's fingers tightened on hers as he said:

"Nobody. Hollingshead is keeping your place open for you. I told you that."

It was a lie, but he spoke convincingly and saw the light come back into her eyes.

"We'll know today, won't we?" Katie asked. "Dr. Medwin felt sure he'd be able to tell us today."

"Yes, that is what he said," Harry agreed.

He was looking at Katie as she lay back against the pillow with her long red-gold hair streaming over her shoulders.

Although the sun was not directly on her, it appeared as if the gold of it illuminated her hair, making the red lights in it glow almost as if they were alive.

"What are you thinking about, Harry?" Katie asked.

"I was thinking how lovely you look."

"What's the point of looking lovely when I'm stuck in here and unable to dance?"

Her voice was raw and as if he wished to change the subject Harry rose to pick up the newspaper which was on the floor by his chair, as he said:

"The Duke of Tregaron is dying."

"I hope he rots in hell!"

"I would agree with you," Harry said, "except that I think it will be a very comfortable hell with special devils to bring him champagne and caviar whenever he wants it."

He thought Katie would smile, but instead she said:

"It isn't fair that he should die in every comfort while I, at my age, have to lie here worrying what you are going to do when there's nothing coming in at the end of the week."

"I told you not to worry about it," Harry said. "I'll manage somehow."

"But how?" Katie asked. "I've got to get back to work, you know that."

"I know, I know!" Harry agreed. "But you can't do anything until we hear what Dr. Medwin has to say."

He glanced down at the newspaper and as if making another effort to divert Katie's mind from herself, he said:

"Tell me about the Duke. I never asked you exactly what he did to you."

"What do you think he did?" Katie retorted. "The dirty old devil! It makes me sick to think of him!"

"You must have been very young when you knew him. We've been together for four years."

"It was six years ago when I first came to London," Katie replied. "I was over the moon at getting a part at the Olympic Music Hall. Only in the chorus at first, but it was my hair which got me a solo."

"What do you mean, your hair?"

"It happened at a rehearsal," Katie answered. "I was dancing with the rest and putting a bit of spirit into it when my hair-pins fell out and my hair tumbled down."

There was a faint smile on her lips as she went on:

"I was embarrassed, but I just carried on with the dance and when it was over I started to pick up my hair-pins. Then the Stage Manager says to me:

" 'You there! Leave your hair as it is and try doing those last steps solo'."

There was a sudden lilt in Katie's voice as she said:

"You can imagine I put some verve into that! Then every night I came on with my hair pinned up and when it tumbled down the audience loved it!"

For a moment Katie was back in the past, then without Harry saying anything, she continued:

"I must have been doing that dance for three weeks when one of the girls says to me:

" 'There's a reel toff in the stage-box tonight'.

"Of course when I goes on, I looks to see what she means and I was disappointed."

"I suppose it was the Duke," Harry commented.

"I didn't know that at first," Katie said, "not until he sends his card round to ask me to have supper with him."

"And you went?"

"Of course I went! The girls were all mad with envy at my eating with a real, live Duke!"

There was a note of triumph in her voice as she continued:

" 'Why should he ask you?' the leading lady says ever so petulant, and the rest more or less echoed the same words."

"I wouldn't have been surprised," Harry said.

Katie smiled at him before she went on:

"When I joins him at the stage-door I wasn't over-impressed. He seemed very old and there was something I didn't like about him. But as I drove off in his carriage, I knew I was moving into a world I didn't even know existed."

"How old were you?"

"Just seventeen," Katie replied, "and I knew nothing about people like him – why should I?"

"Why indeed?" Harry agreed.

"You're a gentleman, you know how people like the Duke behave. To me it was all new – a carriage drawn by two horses, a footman on the box, the Proprietor of the Restaurant almost rupturing himself he bowed so low, the best table, a spray of orchids for me, caviar and champagne which I'd never tasted before."

"You must have drunk champagne!" Harry expostulated.

"Not the sort he brought me! That was something different from the fizz I'd been given in Stockport! And the food! I used to wish I could eat enough to last me for a week!"

"What happened?" Harry asked.

"Nothing that night, and not for several weeks," Katie answered. " 'I'm a good girl, Your Grace,' I says to him when he told me what he wanted."

"What did he say to that?"

"He tried to convince me by saying: 'I can make you very happy and give you comforts you have never had before'."

"But you were firm with him."

"If you mean I didn't let him touch me, that's true enough. I didn't want him to, for one thing. He seemed old and repulsive, but I liked the flowers he gave me and the presents."

"Good ones?"

"I thought so at the time, but when I came to sell them I found he hadn't been all that generous. How was I to judge when before him nobody had given me anything more than an extra drink?"

"Go on," Harry prompted.

"Well, the Duke asks me out, not every night, but about three times a week, and each time he became more persuasive and more insistent until I knew I would have to do what he wanted, which I had no intention of doing, or tell him to get knotted."

"And which did you do?"

"I was trying to make up my mind, but it was difficult because the other girls were all so envious, telling me to string him along. But by this time I'd heard about his reputation."

"I can imagine what you heard."

"I know what you're thinking," Katie said, "but when you're young you're very confident about your ability to handle anybody. So I wasn't really frightened of him, even though we had a couple of struggles in his carriage."

"He didn't suggest taking you anywhere else?"

"Of course he did!

" 'If you dine alone with me, we can be by ourselves,' he used to say.

" 'Oh, no, Your Grace,' I'd reply. 'I want everybody to see how clever I am to be supping with anyone as important as you'."

Harry laughed.

"Fortunately the private rooms in all the Restaurants he patronised were upstairs," Katie went on, "and I refused to put my foot on the first step. His Grace was angry and frustrated, but what could he do about it?"

"Then what happened?" Harry asked.

"I was had for a 'mug'," Katie said with a sigh, "I might have guessed I couldn't keep him at arms' length forever!"

She paused before she explained:

"It was a Saturday night and I'd had a long week. There had also been a Matinée that day. I was tired, and the Duke plied me with champagne. Although I wasn't 'tiddly' I had had enough not to be as sharp-witted as I'd been at other times. Then the Head Waiter comes to our table to say:

" 'Lady Constance's compliments, and she would be delighted if Your Grace and the young lady who is having supper with you would join her party upstairs. Her Ladyship is sure you will find it enjoyable, and there are several famous ladies and gentlemen from the Theatre present.'

"The Duke turns to me and asks:

" 'It will be amusing, and we need not stay long. Who knows it might prove a stepping-stone in your career.'

"I thought it sounded exciting as I'd always wanted to meet some of the leads who were playing in other Theatres.

" 'I'd like to go,' I said.

" 'Will you thank Lady Constance,' the Duke says to the Head Waiter, 'and tell Her Ladyship that Miss King and I will join her as soon as we have finished supper.'

14

" 'Very good, Your Grace.'

"I see the man going up the stairs and it never struck me for one moment, that it was anything but a genuine invitation."

"You mean it was a way the Duke had thought up for enticing you into a private room?" Harry asked.

"That's right," Katie replied. "About ten minutes later we goes up the stairs and the waiter leads us down a dark passage. I could hear people talking and laughing in the rooms we passed, then he opens a door."

There was a sharp note now in Katie's voice which was unmistakable as she continued:

"I walked past him into the room where the lights were low and – it's empty! Being innocent and a bit befuddled with drink, I looks around, and I thought it was an ante-room for where the party was taking place. Then I looked back and see the Duke locking the door and putting the key in his pocket. I knew then I'd been tricked!"

"Was there nothing you could do?" Harry asked.

"I screamed and he hit me!" Katie said simply. "Then the more I struggled the more he seemed to enjoy it. He was very strong and because I'm a coward I didn't put up much resistance after the first frantic efforts of trying to escape."

"Poor Katie!"

"I learned later that half the girls in the Theatre had the same kind of tale to tell. Never trust a toff and never drink if you want to get the better of him! That's my motto for a country girl who goes on the stage!"

"I have always heard the Duke is a swine!" Harry said. "What did he give you?"

"Fifty pounds and there were no more flowers and no more invitations to supper."

"Do you mean that?" Harry asked in surprise.

"There were plenty of people to tell me afterwards that all he wanted was to be the first with someone young,

innocent and untouched, and that's what he got with me!
And cheap at the price!"

Katie's voice was hard.

"He made me loathe all men until you came along, but
you were different. Oh, Harry, I love you!"

"We have had happy times together," Harry said, "and
we will have lots more, you see. When the doctor tells you
the good news, you'll be back on the stage and before you
know where you are Hollingshead will make you his leading lady."

"That's what I want," Katie said. "The lead at the
Gaiety – '*MISS KATIE KING APPEARS IN THE PRINCESS
OF TREBIZONDE!*'"

"That is what it will be, you mark my words!" Harry
said. "You've got another month to get well. They tell me
this Show he brought over from Paris is going to be the
finest we've ever seen. And I have always liked Offenbach's
music."

"I have to be in it, I have to be!" Katie cried.

"You will be," Harry said confidently.

Almost as though he was arriving on cue, they heard a
rap at the door which meant the doctor was outside.

* * *

Harry was standing out on the landing when Dr. Medwin
came out of Katie's room.

He was a middle-aged man with hair beginning to go
grey and the lines on his face and the pallor of his skin
proclaimed that he was both over-worked and under-fed.

He was not only a good doctor, he was a judge of character. Although he knew Harry Carrington for what he was,
a man who lived off the earnings of the women to whom
he made love, he still liked him.

He was a ne'er-do-well, a man who had never done a
day's work in his life, but he was a gentleman by birth and
he had a charm that for women was inescapable.

He also, Dr. Medwin thought, had the decency to stand
by Katie King at this moment in her life when, if she had

been left alone with her own fears, she might easily have killed herself.

The Thames which formed the northern boundary of Dr. Medwin's large practice in Lambeth had received several of his patients who could not face life after they knew the truth about their health.

Harry was leaning over the rickety banisters as Dr. Medwin came out of Katie's room, shutting the door firmly behind him.

"What is the verdict?" Harry asked tensely.

"Bad!"

"That is what I expected."

"So did I, but I had to have it confirmed. The tests show undoubtedly a cancerous growth."

"What can you do about it?"

"Very little, I am afraid."

Dr. Medwin sighed.

"It seems terrible to say that of a woman who is not much over twenty-three years of age and who is as lovely as Katie King."

"Surely there must be something you can do?"

"I can make sure she does not suffer too much, but I will not pretend to you that the pains will not grow more and more acute and only drugs will keep her from experiencing the full agony of them."

"Is that all?" Harry asked in a dull voice.

"If you were rich I could give you a different answer," Dr. Medwin said. "There is new hope for those who undergo surgery which was raised about five years ago, by the revolutionary ideas of a man called Joseph Lister."

"I believe I have read about him."

"He has written a paper on his belief that antiseptics can prevent putrefaction in surgical wounds and his theories are borne out by what a man called Louis Pasteur is saying in France."

"And yet this does not apply in Katie's case?"

"Where Miss King is concerned," Dr. Medwin said, "the

only thing I can do is to send her to one of our local Hospitals, where there is a bed available."

He paused before he went on :

"They admit that the chance of coming out alive after any operation is not more than 50/50, but I can assure you, from my personal experience, it is far less."

"That is what I have heard," Harry said savagely, "and I wouldn't let an animal endure the conditions to be found in those hospitals."

"Exactly !" Dr. Medwin agreed.

Both men were silent and Dr. Medwin was thinking about sepsis and how often he had to watch the skin and flesh round a wound become red, hot and swollen.

Gradually it would turn black with gangrene, foul-smelling fluid and pus would seep out and the patient would shiver, run a high fever, and it would all end in death.

It was as if Harry had followed his thoughts, for he asked :

"You say there is an alternative ?"

"There is one Surgeon at the moment who is working on Lister's methods and has his own private Nursing Home."

"What is his name ?"

"Sheldon Curtis, and he is not only a first class Surgeon but by using carbolic acid as an antiseptic, during and after surgery, I am told that he has cut the deaths that occur of those in his hands, to fewer than five per cent."

There was silence, then Harry asked tersely :

"How much does he charge ?"

"With his Nursing Home fees he would not consider a patient at under £200."

Harry gave a short laugh with no humour in it.

"At the moment I hardly have that amount in shillings."

"Then as I have said," Dr. Medwin remarked, "I will do my best to keep Miss King from suffering."

"And what is she to do in the meantime ?"

"Anything she likes, but she will not feel like moving

18

about very much, and certainly not dancing. I am sorry, Carrington, but I knew you would prefer to know the truth."

"Yes, of course."

"It is no consolation," Dr. Medwin added, "but I am about to have this same conversation with another patient whose condition I had tested at the same time as Miss King's. I expect you have heard of him – he lives a little way up the road – Professor Braintree."

"I seem to have read about him somewhere," Harry remarked.

"A brilliant man, admired as an authority on 13th century literature by everybody in the intellectual world, which unfortunately does not make them buy his books."

Dr. Medwin picked up his black bag which he had put down on the floor while he was talking to Harry.

"Strangely enough, his daughter had hair of the same colour as Miss King's. I think it is an extraordinary co-incidence that I should have two patients with hair that is almost unique and I can never remember seeing a woman with it until now."

"It does seem strange," Harry agreed. "In fact like you, until I met Katie, I didn't know such a colour existed except on the canvas of some old master."

"It is beautiful, absolutely beautiful!" Dr. Medwin said with a note of enthusiasm in his tired voice. "It is a pity, a great pity we cannot do more for Miss King, or for Miss Braintree's father."

He started to walk down the stairs and Harry followed him.

"What you are saying," he said, "is that if Professor Braintree had the money, he could be operated on by this man Curtis and he could be saved, as Katie could."

"There is always a chance of course, that the cancer may have gone too far," Dr. Medwin answered cautiously, "but if you want my professional opinion, both Miss King and the Professor could be saved if they could be operated on immediately, and by Sheldon Curtis."

He had reached the narrow, rather dirty Hall and paused before he opened the front door.

"I already know the answer," he said, "but I have to ask you whether, after all I have said, you would like to take the risk of sending Miss King to hospital."

"You know my reply to that," Harry said. "If I thought she had the slightest chance I would jump at it, but I have heard of too many people dying in Hospital after they have been butchered. If she has to die, let her die cleanly."

"I thought you would say that," Dr. Medwin answered. "Goodbye, Carrington, I wish I could have brought you better news. I will call in a day or so. Send for me if she is in any great pain."

"Yes, of course," Harry replied, "and thank you."

The Doctor lifted his hand in acknowledgement, walked down the broken steps and turned towards another part of the neighbourhood where the houses were a little better than the one in which Katie lodged.

Harry walked very slowly back up the stairs to the second floor.

Outside Katie's door he paused before he opened it and with a considerable effort before he went in, forced a smile to his lips.

"What did he say? He wouldn't tell me. He said he'd tell you," Katie said.

She was sitting up higher on her pillows, and with her red-gold hair falling below her waist she looked so lovely that for a moment Harry could only stare at her and wonder if it was possible that he had just heard her sentenced to death.

Then with a smile he said:

"The Doctor was very encouraging. Things are not as bad as he thought and he is coming again in a few days. He says by that time he is sure you will feel better."

"Did he really say that? Really and truly?" Katie asked.

Harry sat down on the bed and put his arms around her.

"Do you think I would tell you a lie," he asked. "You have to get well, darling, and quickly, or we are going to be very hungry, you and I!"

"Oh, Harry, once I am back on the stage I will work so hard that we'll soon be living in luxury, and you can have that new suit you need."

Katie could say no more because Harry was kissing her.

Then as he felt her go limp in his arms he knew he had excited her and said:

"I am not going to tire you, darling, not tonight, at any rate. I am happy just to look at you. The Doctor said just now how lovely you are."

"They'll be clapping me again when I go on the stage with my hair hanging down," Katie said in a rapt little voice.

"The Doctor was saying he would have called it a unique colour," Harry said, as if he spoke to himself, "if there was not another girl just up the road whose hair is the same."

"I don't believe it!" Katie cried. "She got it out of a dye-pot!"

"Not according to the Doctor."

"I'll scratch her eyes out if her hair's prettier than mine!"

"Don't worry, my precious! There couldn't be anyone with hair like yours."

"That's what the dirty old Duke said! An Enchantress, he called me. He used to write cards to go with the flowers saying: 'To an Enchantress who draws me with every hair on her exquisite head!'"

Katie laughed and asked:

"Do you know what he said to me once?"

"What did he say?" Harry enquired without much interest in his voice.

"He said: 'I have had three wives and outlived them all, and I would give any woman who could produce a son for me half my fortune, besides making her my Duchess.' "

"Three wives! From the way he behaved, he doesn't deserve to propagate his own species!" Harry exclaimed.

He saw Katie's expression and asked:

"Did you wonder if he had given you a baby?"

"Of course I did," Katie answered, "but he was so bestial and so brutal, and I didn't believe babies are born that way."

"Nevertheless if you had produced a boy you could have been a Duchess."

"I'd rather be with you, you old stupid!" Katie laughed.

She put out her hands towards him.

"You deserve a slap-up time after this, my Harry, and I'll see you have it, if it's the last thing I do!"

She took his hand and held it in both of hers.

"Today's our lucky day," she said. "Who knows? Perhaps when that old devil's dead we'll hear that he left me something in his will."

Harry laughed. Then suddenly he was tense, and Katie felt his fingers stiffen.

"What is it?"

"I have an idea!" Harry replied.

"What?"

"I will tell you later, but I think there might be something which will bring us the luck we've always needed."

"Oh, tell me, Harry!"

"No, I've got to think it out."

"I'll die of curiosity!"

It flashed through Harry's mind that she would die of cancer unless his idea was practical.

He rose to his feet.

"I am going out," he said. "I'll not be long."

"I told you to go out and get some air," Katie said. "While you're gone, I'll have a snooze."

"That's sensible."

Harry bent down to kiss her on the cheek.

"You're so kind to me, Harry," Katie said softly with a

little sob in her voice. "I don't know what I'd do without you. You'll come back, won't you?"

"I am not going to answer such a ridiculous question," he answered, "and I'll buy something nice for supper."

"With what?" Katie asked automatically. Then she said:

"What about pawning my coat? By the time I'm up and about, I shan't need it, and that old Shylock ought to give you a pound or more for it."

Harry hesitated. Then he said:

"All right. As you say, the weather will be warm next month and when you are well enough to go back to the Theatre you could ask for your wages in advance."

"Of course," Katie agreed. "The coat's hanging up behind the curtain, and before you go, could you give me a handkerchief? I think there's one in my top drawer."

Harry went to the rough deal chest-of-drawers which stood in one corner of the room.

He opened the drawer and saw that it was filled with a miscellaneous collection of ribbons, handkerchiefs, artificial flowers, and some tattered scarves.

He found a handkerchief and as he drew it out, he said:

"Did the Duke write you any letters?"

"He was always sending me notes telling me what time he'd be calling to take me out to supper. It was more of an order than an invitation. He never expected a girl to refuse anyone as important as himself."

"Did you keep them?"

"Oh, I expect so. I keep everything. My mother used to say I was a born hoarder."

"Where are they?"

"In the bottom drawer, with the programmes of the Shows I've been in and the newspaper reviews. I've always kept them. I was actually mentioned in one or two."

"You are sure there are letters from the Duke?"

"I think so, and there are the cards he used to send me with the flowers saying: 'To my Enchantress!' If I'd

23

known what he was really like I'd have burned the lot!"

"But you didn't?" Harry asked quickly.

"No, I was too lazy. Besides, when I was famous I was going to put in my autobiography: *'SEDUCED BY A DUKE!'* It sounds like a title of a novelette, doesn't it?"

Harry took her coat from behind the curtain. It had a collar of cheap fur and looked very different on the hanger than it did when Katie wore it.

"Ta-ta, darling! Don't be long!" she said from the bed.

"I'll be as quick as I can," Harry replied. "You have a sleep, and that, by the way, is an order, even if it's not a Ducal one!"

He heard her laugh as he shut the door.

*   *   *

"Larentia!"

"I am coming, Papa!"

Larentia Braintree picked up the coffee she had been making in the kitchen to climb the stairs to her father's bedroom.

It was a pleasant room with two windows overlooking the road and the ceiling was fairly high, as they were all over the tall house that was far too big for them, but they could not afford to move.

"I have made you some coffee, Papa."

"I dropped one of my papers on the floor," Professor Braintree replied. "I am sorry to drag you upstairs, dearest, but I need it."

"I wish you would stop working, Papa, and rest."

Even as she spoke she thought with a slight constriction of her heart, that it did not matter what he did. Dr. Medwin had said:

"Do not tell him the truth. Let him believe he is getting better until the truth is forced upon him."

"Will he .. suffer very acutely?" Larentia had asked.

"I will try to prevent the worst pains," the Doctor replied, "but you realise the drugs will have to be stronger

24

and stronger until it will be impossible for him to think or even recognise you."

Larentia had gone very pale, but she had not cried out and the Doctor had admired her self-control.

"You must do what is .. best for Papa," she said. "Is there no other way we can .. save him?"

"There is just a chance if he goes to hospital, Miss Braintree."

"No! Not the hospital!" Larentia said in a horrified tone. "I have heard too many stories from the people round here of what they have suffered or rather their relatives have. The death rate is appalling!"

"I agree with you," Dr. Medwin said. "That is why, because I have the greatest admiration and respect for your father, Miss Braintree, I would rather he died in his own bed."

"So would I," Larentia agreed, "but .. is there .. no other way?"

Slowly, feeling for words, the Doctor explained, as he had explained to Harry, that the only hope was to pay a Surgeon like Sheldon Curtis who used Lister's methods of keeping the wound from a surgical operation from becoming infected.

"I have heard of this Mr. Lister," Larentia said, in her soft voice, "and Papa was very interested in the work he has been doing in Edinburgh."

"It is revolutionary!" Dr. Medwin agreed. He paused before he added:

"I suppose there is no chance, Miss Braintree, that you could find the £200 that would be required if I was to approach Mr. Sheldon Curtis on your father's behalf?"

Larentia made a helpless little gesture with her hands.

"It would be impossible for us to find anything like that amount of money," she said. "Papa's relations are mostly dead, and those who are living are as impoverished as we are ourselves."

She thought for a moment before she went on:

"As you may be aware, we do not own this house, we only rent it, and we have nothing valuable to sell which would fetch anything like that sum of money."

"I was afraid of that."

"Papa was still in the middle of his latest book and, even if it was finished, I doubt if the publishers would give him a very big advance on it."

She made a sound that was curiously like a groan.

"The things they write about Papa in the newspapers are very flattering, but his books do not sell because they are too clever and few people would want to read about mediaeval times or even his treatise on King Arthur, a legendary hero who has always fascinated me."

"And me, when I have time to think about him," Dr. Medwin said, with a smile.

He looked at Larentia and thought how beautiful she was.

Katie King had the flamboyant prettiness that is associated with the stage, and when she was well, her sparkling eyes, her laughing red mouth and her pert, turned-up nose made every man who saw her turn his head to look again.

Larentia Braintree had a different kind of beauty.

Her features were almost classically perfect and her large eyes, which had a glint of green in them, were soft and gentle, and gave her face a kind of spiritual loveliness which the Doctor had never seen before.

He found himself wondering if her hair was as long as Katie King's, then told himself he was too busy to have time to think about young women, however attractive they might be.

"I must get back to work, Miss Braintree," he said. "Forgive me for bringing you such bad news. I only wish I could be optimistic and tell you that your father will recover."

"He must never know," Larentia said, almost in a whisper. "I shall tell him you are certain he will soon be back on his feet again and when you next call on us, you must say the same thing."

"You are your father's daughter," Dr. Medwin said. "I admire you as I admire him, and I will do anything in my power to prevent him from suffering."

"Thank .. you."

There was just a little sob in her voice and her eyes were moist.

She blinked the tears away and saw the Doctor to the door before she went into the kitchen to make her father the coffee he enjoyed when he was working.

Now as she picked up the piece of paper he had dropped she put it in front of him, then sat down in a chair looking at him as if she saw him for the first time.

No-one, she thought, could have a more distinguished-looking father. His grey hair brushed back from the square forehead and his fine features seemed to belong to another age and always entranced her.

She could understand how her mother had fallen in love with him when they first met and her father had felt the same.

"Your mother was very beautiful," he had said to Larentia hundreds of times when they had been talking about the woman they had both loved. "She had Hungarian blood in her, which I suppose accounts for the beauty of her hair which was like yours, but a little deeper in colour. I used to tell her she should have been painted by Boucher."

"She always seemed to me to be like a Fairy Princess," Larentia said. "I remember sometimes when you were going out to dinner together that I used to think that wherever you went people would stop talking just to look at you both."

Her father had laughed. Then he had said with a serious note in his voice:

"Can you imagine what it meant to me possessing nothing of value but my brain when your mother said she would marry me?"

"I remember her telling me that," Larentia said, "and she told me that the only thing that mattered in the world was love, and she was a millionairess a million times over because you loved her."

She saw how much her words pleased her father.

"I have done some good work today," he said now, "but I do feel a little tired, Larentia."

"Drink your coffee, Papa, then try to rest. It has been a lovely afternoon and I want to sit in the garden, but I will not be long in case you need me."

"You are not to go out into the street alone at this time of the evening," the Professor said.

"Of course not, Papa. You know I promised you I would never do that."

"You should have somebody with you always," the Professor murmured, almost beneath his breath, "but how can we pay for a servant at the moment?"

His eyes were anxious as he added:

"When this book is finished I am sure it will make more than any of my others. My new research on Arthur is quite different from what I have done before. In fact, I feel it important that Alfred Tennyson should know what I have recently unearthed."

"I believe Mr. Tennyson has been living in the Isle of Wight ever since he married," Larentia said coldly.

She did not wish her father to know how deeply she resented the fact that twelve years ago when Alfred Tennyson was working on *The Idylls of the King* he had consulted her father and visited him continually.

Then, when the book had been published, he had forgotten all about the assistance he had received from the greatest expert on that subject.

Because her father had been hurt by the indifference of the man whose work he admired, they had never spoken of Alfred Tennyson. But now it flashed through Larentia's mind that she might ask for his assistance.

The Charge of the Light Brigade must have brought Mr. Tennyson in a fortune, she told herself.

She knew that *The Holy Grail and other poems* had been published this year, but she could not afford to buy her father a copy, so she did not mention it to him in case she made him curious.

"I expect Alfred Tennyson has completely forgotten Papa's existence," she told herself bitterly.

Then looking at the serene, handsome face of her father she thought she would not have him upset or worried by the treachery of his friends or enemies.

"When you have had a rest, Papa, I will bring you up your supper, and while you are eating it, I will read aloud what you have written today. I am sure it will be very exciting, and I shall enjoy every word."

"You always encourage me, my dearest," the Professor replied.

Then as she took the empty cup from him to lay it down on the tray she thought he was, in fact, very tired and the effort of writing grew heavier for him every day.

"You are not in..pain, Papa?" she asked, finding it difficult to say the words.

"Only a little, a very little. It is nothing," the Professor replied testily.

Larentia did not say any more. She walked across the room to pull down the blind a little and shut out the evening sun.

Then as she walked carefully down the stairs, carrying the empty coffee cup on a tray, she heard a knock on the front door and wondered who it could be.

"Suppose," she told herself, "it is a letter from the publishers telling Papa that unexpectedly they have sold a great many more copies of his last book!"

Then she knew that it was just a fancy.

The book he had written on King Arthur, translated from the Welsh poem 'Y *Gododdin*' had not sold for over a year, which meant that the Libraries already had all they needed and the public were not interested.

As she reached the foot of the stairs the knock came again and as she walked towards the door she wondered who could be in such a hurry that they could not wait for her to answer their summons.

Chapter Two

Larentia opened the door and to her surprise saw a gentleman she had never seen before.

Most of her father's friends were elderly, but this man, although not young, was certainly not in that category.

Then because she was observant she noticed that while he appeared outwardly smart there were signs of poverty.

The over-polished shoes to hide the cracks, the starched cuffs of his shirt trimmed at the edges, and a tie which was definitely worn at the knot.

Then she realised that the caller was staring at her in astonishment.

It was something she was used to, but not in quite such an obvious manner.

Then as she waited he found his voice.

"You are Miss Braintree?"

"Yes."

"I wonder if it would be possible for me to speak to you for a moment, privately? I am a friend of Dr. Medwin's."

Larentia gave him a little smile.

"Dr. Medwin is an old friend of my father's."

"I am aware of that, and it is about your father I wish to talk to you."

Larentia opened the door wider and Harry Carrington stepped into the hall.

She appeared to hesitate for a moment, then she said in a low voice:

"My father is resting and if he hears us talking here he may not sleep as I wish him to do. I was going into the garden."

"Then I should be very glad to accompany you," Harry said.

She smiled at him again and he told himself that never in his life had he seen anyone so beautiful, and with the same colour hair as Katie's, but which embellished Larentia in a different way.

He found it difficult to put into words, but there was about this girl, he thought, something he had never found in a woman, and as he followed her into the garden he tried to think what it was.

"Katie must have looked like this when she first came to London," he told himself and found the word he was seeking. It was 'pure'.

He thought that garden was a rather pretentious name for what was little more than a plot of ground bordered by a wall which protected it from being seen from the road and which contained one acacia tree and a few rather tired-looking shrubs.

But there was a wooden seat with its back to the house and when Larentia sat down on it the sunshine illuminated her hair and gave the whole garden a beauty which had not been there before.

Harry seated himself beside her.

When he took off his hat and put it down on the ground beside him, she noticed that his hair was greased back from his rather low forehead and had the same kind of shine as was on his shoes.

She wondered what he could possibly have to say to her and whether, as he was a friend of Dr. Medwin, he also belonged to the world of medicine.

Then as if he had been feeling for words, Harry began :

"You must not think me impertinent, Miss Braintree, when I say how deeply sorry I am to hear of your father's illness."

He noted the stricken look which came into Larentia's eyes, but she only replied in a low voice :

"Thank you. If you speak to my father please do not

mention it. He has no idea how .. ill he is."

"I know Dr. Medwin's methods too well to do that,"
Harry answered. "He gives his patients hope up to the last
moment."

"I am sure that is the right thing to do."

"I think Dr. Medwin will have told you," Harry went
on, "that if you could afford it there might be a chance of
saving your father's life by being operated on by Mr.
Sheldon Curtis."

He saw unhappiness in Larentia's eyes, although she
merely replied :

"That is what he said, but it is .. impossible."

"Just as it is impossible for a friend of mine who should
be treated in the same way."

"Your friend has .. cancer?"

The question was almost inaudible as if Larentia was
afraid to speak the word.

"So Dr. Medwin has found," Harry replied. "But he
offered me, as I know he has offered you, the choice of two
alternatives, either to go into Hospital, or to find the
money for the only Surgeon who could save her life."

Larentia drew in her breath.

"That is exactly what he told me about Papa, but I
cannot think how we could possibly find such a sum and
so .. there is nothing I can do but look after him and hope
he does not .. suffer .. too m . much."

Her voice broke on the last words and she clenched her
hands together as if with an effort at self-control.

Harry nodded his head.

"My friend is in exactly the same position. Her name
is Katie King, and she was an actress, or rather a dancer,
at the Gaiety."

"I am very sorry for her."

"She is only twenty-three, and she does not want to
die!"

"It is cruel! Surely someone some day will find a cure
for this ghastly .. disease."

"We must hope so," Harry said gravely. "In the meantime, I want to save Katie King, and you want to save your father. I have an idea, with your help, how it could be done."

Larentia's eyes widened.

"I would do anything .. anything to .. save Papa."

"That is what I hoped you would say," Harry replied, "but I have to ask you, Miss Braintree, if you can act."

"Act? Do you mean on the stage?"

"Not exactly on the stage, but nevertheless pretend that you are another person and play the part so cleverly that you can make people believe that you are whom you pretend to be."

"I do not .. think I .. understand."

"Have you ever acted a part at School or anywhere else?"

"I am afraid not. But I have read my father's lectures for him when he has had a sore throat to which he is prone in the winter."

"Good!" Harry exclaimed. "That means you are not nervous."

"Not really, although it is rather frightening to read to scholars or students who are very critical of how one pronounces the more obscure words, especially when they are written in Latin or Welsh!"

Harry looked surprised, but he did not wish to deviate from what she was saying, so he merely went on :

"I think we have established, Miss Braintree, that you could, especially if you were determined to do so, play the part of a woman who has been wronged."

He paused as if he expected Larentia to speak, and after a moment she said a little hesitatingly :

"Will you .. please explain what .. you are .. asking me to do?"

"What I am really asking is that you should obtain enough money to pay for an operation that will give both your father and Katie King a chance to live out their lives normally rather than dying in agony."

He heard Larentia draw in her breath as if the thought of it hurt her and he went on :

"Six years ago when she was only seventeen the Duke of Tregaron married Katie King because he thought she would give him the son he was so desperately anxious to have."

He looked at Larentia and realised she was listening intently before he continued :

"When she did not produce a child he left her, and because their wedding had been secret, he paid her a certain sum of money every year never to reveal that the marriage had taken place."

Harry gave an exclamation of exasperation, before he said :

"Of course, because she was young and foolish, she agreed to his terms, which were far from generous. In fact the Duke being a very unpleasant man, they were extremely mean. But because she is honourable and straightforward she had never gone back on her word, and it is only recently that I who am closer to her than anybody else, learned that she is, in reality, the Duchess of Tregaron."

"Surely in that case she can afford to have the operation!" Larentia exclaimed.

"It is not as easy as that," Harry answered. "You see, the Duke has been ill for some time, in fact the papers say he is dying, and in consequence Katie's money has not arrived and she is uncertain as to whether she will ever receive any again."

"But that is wrong!" Larentia said. "Surely she can apply to the Duke's lawyers?"

Harry shook his head.

"I told you, Katie is a very honourable person. She gave the Duke her word of honour, or rather he extracted it from her, that she would never speak of their marriage to anyone except himself. Because she has accepted the money for the last six years she feels that even in her extremity she must not betray him now."

"That is very noble of her," Larentia remarked.

"I thought you would think so," Harry replied.

"But .. what are you asking .. me to .. do?"

"I am asking you," Harry said, "to go to Tregaron Castle and ask a member of the family for the money that is rightfully Katie's."

"But surely she could do that herself? Or if she is not well enough, you could do it for her."

"I am asking you, Miss Braintree, because you and Katie have the same colour hair and look somewhat alike, to pretend that you are in fact the Duchess of Tregaron!"

Harry spoke very quietly, but to Larentia it was as if he had set off a bomb at her feet.

She stared at him incredulously. Then she said in a voice that was hardly audible:

"You are .. asking me to .. claim I am the .. Duke's wife?"

"By the time you get there he will be the late Duke," Harry replied, "so there is no chance of his recognising you are not the woman he married."

"I could not .. do that .. how could I?"

There was silence. Then Harry said in a rather different tone of voice:

"Perhaps I was mistaken, but I thought you loved your father."

"I do! Of course I do! He is everything I have in the whole world!"

"Then this is the only way you can save his life."

"But .. I would not be able to .. act a lie .. I would be .. unconvincing .. I could not do it .. it is impossible!"

Harry bent forward to pick up his hat from the ground.

"You must forgive me, Miss Braintree," he said, "for wasting your time. I had just a forlorn hope that you might be brave enough to save two people from dying. I regret having troubled you."

He would have walked away, but Larentia gave a little cry.

"No .. please .. please .. sit down and let me .. think! What you have suggested is a .. shock!"

With what appeared to be reluctance Harry seated himself again, but he held his hat in his hand as if at any moment he was prepared to put it back on his head.

After a moment Larentia said in a voice that trembled:

"How could I .. convince the Duke's relatives .. or whoever I speak to, that I am the .. Duchess?"

"You can take with you Miss King's Marriage Certificate, and a letter from the Duke which refers to their marriage. In it he says how much he hopes that she will give him a son."

"How .. how old is Miss King .. now?"

"As I told you, she is twenty-three. She looks very young and I am sure it will not be difficult for you to appear to be the same age."

"No .. I suppose not."

"I will of course, tell you of that Music Hall Katie was performing when she met the Duke, and I will give you the names of the Restaurants where they had supper, the Shows in which she has appeared since at the Gaiety Theatre. But there is no need to tell you, Miss Braintree, that it would be a mistake to talk too much about yourself."

"Yes .. yes .. of course."

"What I want you to do, is to go to Tregaron Castle and ask to see the oldest of the Duke's many relatives. I will look up their names for you but I happen to know that one of his sisters is the Dowager Marchioness of Humber. I can't remember any others at the moment."

Harry frowned a little as he concentrated, then as if it was of no consequence went on:

"You will show the Marchioness the papers I will give you and I am certain she will be shocked and horrified by the fact that the Duke had a secret life of which none of them were aware."

"Suppose they .. turn me out of the house?" Larentia asked.

"They are not likely to do that when you can prove that you are the Duke's wife."

"Suppose they .. tear up the Marriage .. Certificate?"

"The Marriage will be recorded in the Church in which it took place," Harry said, "but I do not think the Dowager Marchioness is likely to behave in such an uncontrolled fashion. No, what she will do, Miss Braintree, is to pay up."

"Will that mean I will be given quite a large sum of money?"

"A very large sum!" Harry said firmly, "for the simple reason that you are not going to ask for the small annual allowance which the Duke paid his wife, but for a substantial capital payment in return for which you will promise to disappear out of their lives for ever."

"All we really want is enough for the two operations," Larentia said quickly.

"Katie wants a great deal more than that," Harry replied. "Can you imagine what her position has been like, knowing that because she was married to the Duke when she was too young to know what she was doing, she could never marry anybody else?"

Harry made his voice sound very confidential as he said:

"I do not mind telling you that because she is so beautiful, like yourself, she has had some marvellous offers from men who have watched her dance and afterwards fallen in love with her."

He sighed and asked:

"But what could she do but refuse them without an explanation, leaving them bewildered, and in many cases bitter, because they could not understand why she would not make them happy?"

"I can see it was a very unfortunate predicament to be .. in."

"Now, on top of everything else, when she has a golden future in front of her on the stage, she has been stricken down in a way which would make you weep to see her."

There was a throb in Harry's voice which was very moving.

"I am .. sorry .. very .. very sorry."

"Just as Katie was sorry for you when she heard that your father must die unless we save them both."

"Are you quite .. certain that I shall not .. let you down?" Larentia asked.

"Having met you, Miss Braintree," Harry replied, "I can see that you are not only beautiful, but as intelligent as your father."

"Although it is not true, you could not say anything that would please me more," Larentia said, "but what you ask is a very .. frightening thing to do. Besides, what .. explanation will I make to Papa?"

"I have been thinking about that," Harry replied, "and what I have to do first, is to borrow the money for your father's and Katie's operation because, as I expect Dr. Medwin has told you, the sooner it is performed, the more chance there is of its being successful."

"You mean," Larentia said, a sudden light in her eyes, "that Papa would be able to go to Mr. Curtis immediately?"

"As soon as I can get the money," Harry answered. "But if you agree to do what I ask you, I shall have to bring one person to see you. He is not a very prepossessing creature, but he is rich, and if he lends us money we have of course, to pay him back."

"Of course," Larentia agreed.

Then she looked at him and said shrewdly:

"I feel, Mr. Carrington, you are talking about a Usurer .. a money-lender."

"I said you were intelligent, Miss Braintree."

"Papa has always told me such men are dangerous and demand a very high rate of interest for any money they lend."

"There is no alternative but to pay what he asks," Harry said firmly, "and if the operations are successful, does it matter?"

"No, of course not," Larentia agreed. "How much do you want me to ask for?"

"Five thousand pounds!"

Harry realised as he spoke, that he had taken Larentia's breath away.

"Five thousand .. pounds?" she stammered. "It would be .. impossible for me to .. ask for so .. much."

Harry smiled.

"The Duke of Tregaron doubtless spends more than that on his race-horses every year. He is an immensely rich man with estates all over the country. He owns works of art which are unequalled anywhere. I am quite certain that rather than have the scandal in the family of a Duchess who has been a chorus-girl, they will be only too ready to pay."

There was a hard note in Harry's voice as he added:

"Can you imagine if the Duke had acknowledged Katie as his wife what she would be entitled to, when he dies?"

"Of course .. I understand."

"What I am going to suggest," Harry went on, "is that when we have paid back the money we have borrowed, you will be entitled to a third of what is left."

"You are quite certain that Miss King will not mind my taking so much?" Larentia asked.

"I know that Katie King will be extremely grateful to you for saving her life, as you are saving your father's. Once she can get back to work nothing else will be of any consequence. You have your father to think of, Miss Braintree, for I doubt if, for some time after the operation, he will be able to work."

"Thank you," Larentia said, "but please try to ensure that I .. make no .. mistakes."

Harry smiled.

"I promise you that your script will be well written. I will go over it with you in great detail so that you can ask me questions about anything of which you are uncertain. All you have to do is to have confidence in yourself, Miss Braintree. That is important for any actress, whatever part she undertakes."

"Then .. I will try," Larentia said humbly, "but I am very .. nervous .. and I am sure I will make .. many mistakes."

"Not as many as Katie King would do in the same position. Remember that your background is very different from hers."

He saw the question in Larentia's eyes and said:

"I will tell you everything about her and her struggle to get into the Gaiety, but what I have to do now is to arrange to borrow the money and hand it over to Dr. Medwin, so that he can get both your father and Katie to the Surgeon as quickly as possible."

"That is all that matters," Larentia agreed, "because I can see Papa .. deteriorating a little every .. day!"

"Just like Katie," Harry said, almost under his breath.

He rose to his feet and held out his hand.

"Do not look so worried, Miss Braintree," he said. "I know you are going to be magnificent, and when you are thinking not of yourself but of the people we both love, then you will find it far easier than it seems now."

"I hope so," Larentia said simply.

But when she put her hand in his, Harry was aware that she was trembling.

* * *

Dinner in the *Comte* de Roques' palatial house in the Champs Élysées had been delectable, and the conversation had been stimulating and extremely amusing.

Justin Garon had enjoyed himself more, he thought, than he had done for a long time.

He had always found the wit and quick repartee of the French different from the somewhat ponderous conversation which took place at English dinner-parties.

There was, moreover, a diversion this evening in that the *Comtesse* de Roques was making it very clear that she was prepared to offer him a very different amusement from what was taking place round her husband's dinner-table.

She was very attractive with a *joie de vivre* which was characteristic of the French, and Justin Garon had been aware on the last two occasions they had met that she had singled him out as a recipient of her very exceptional favours.

Although he was a friend of her husband's, he realised that he would not be betraying the *Comte* in any way, if he became his wife's lover.

All Paris knew that the *Comte* was spending his time and his money on the alluring Madame Mustard, who was in the forefront of the famous *demi-mondaines* whose extravagances had shocked Europe.

In what was known as the 'Second Empire' high society paraded their liaisons.

The Emperor made no secret of his love-affairs, and his cousin Prince Napoleon flaunted his mistresses for all to see.

Madame Mustard owed her vast wealth to her infatuated lover, the King of the Netherlands.

His Majesty, however, occasionally had to return to rule over his own country, and the *Comte* de Roques took his place in adding to Madame's enormous fortune, providing her with horses, carriages and jewellery which already exceeded that owned by any other lady of *la vie galante*.

Justin Garon was seated on the *Comtesse*'s right and under the noise of the general conversation, which being on the subject of politics made everyone's voices rise a little higher than usual, she said :

"Will you dine with me tomorrow night?"

"Can you tolerate my company again so soon?" Justin Garon asked.

He knew the answer before he asked the question and there was a decided expression of amusement in his eyes and a twist to his lips.

The *Comtesse* was extremely alluring, but like most Englishmen he preferred to do his own hunting.

"Jacques will be away," the *Comtesse* answered, "and I thought we might have a *tête-à-tête*."

There was no doubt from the look she gave him what this entailed, but as Justin wondered what he should reply, the *Comte* asked his opinion on some argument which was dividing the diners, and the moment of intimacy was lost.

Later that evening the *Comte* said to his friend:

"There is something I want to show you, Justin – something I know you admire but which you will see here in this house for the last time."

For a moment Justin Garon did not understand what he was talking about. Then as they walked towards one of the Salons they were not using that evening he knew the *Comte* was taking him to look at a picture that had always been his favourite in all de Roques' collection.

In fact, he never came to Paris without asking if he could look at it.

He was not mistaken when they walked into the empty Salon to find the newly installed gas-lamps were lit and they shone on a picture called '*Le Bain de Diane*' by Francis Boucher.

It was a picture which thrilled Justin Garon anew everytime he looked at it.

The Goddess Diana with her exquisite, classical little nose in profile was seated naked on a background of blue silk – the colour which the painter had made peculiarly his own.

It threw into prominence the exquisite tones of her flesh and most of all the wonder of her red-gold hair.

The whole picture with Diana's attendant crouching beside her was so perfect in every particular, such a superb portrait of ideal beauty, that Justin Garon stood in front of it feeling as if Diana herself reached out and gave him something personal which he took to his very heart.

Only after he had looked at the picture for some minutes did he ask:

"Did you say I will not see it here again?"

"I have sold it," the *Comte* replied.

"How can you possibly do that?"

"*Le Musée du Louvre* has offered me a good price, and I need the money."

For one moment Justin Garon felt like telling his friend that he was a damned fool.

How could he sell something so priceless, simply in order to squander the money he obtained for it on a woman who extorted money from her lovers as a tribute to her own ego?

He had a strange feeling that he wanted to say that Boucher's Diana could never be sold for money, but only for love.

Then he thought his friend Jacques would not understand.

They both stood in silence, almost as if they were at a shrine, looking at Diana, at the crescent on her forehead, and the curves of her body which had not yet come to full maturity.

"I shall miss it," the *Comte* said with a little sigh.

"And so shall I," Justin Garon replied.

He felt that Diana would never look the same against the impersonal background of a Museum. Her loveliness needed a home, somewhere more intimate, where the atmosphere was fitting for her softness and her femininity.

Then Justin Garon told himself he was being ridiculous and was thinking of Diana as if she was a human being instead of just a mythical figure, painted by a man who had a vision of beauty unsurpassed by any other artist who portrayed woman.

He walked out of the Salon and, as he did so, he told himself it would be impossible for him to make love to the

Comtesse in a house where the woman who embodied all his dreams was in another room.

It was difficult to think how he could explain that it would be impossible for him to accept the invitation for the *tête-à-tête* dinner for tomorrow night, or any other night for that matter.

Then as they reached the hall and were proceeding towards the Salon where the rest of the guests were assembled, a servant came to Justin Garon's side.

"*Pardon, Monsieur*, but there is somebody here to see you. He asked to speak to you, *Monsieur*, in the antechamber."

The servant opened a door and as Justin Garon walked in, he saw a man he recognised and knew why he had come.

* * *

Starting off on what she knew was a long journey Larentia felt more frightened than she had ever been in her whole life.

One part of her mind was singing with happiness because yesterday afternoon she had taken her father to Mr. Sheldon Curtis's Nursing Home in North London.

He had been given a small room, and the Nurse who was to look after him was an elderly woman with a kind face.

The moment Larentia met Mr. Sheldon Curtis she knew that she could trust him.

When she said goodbye to her father Mr. Curtis had asked her to speak with him in his private office.

"You are not to worry, Miss Braintree," he said. "Dr. Medwin has told me all about your father and I have no reason to doubt that in three or four weeks I will send him back to you with every prospect of his living for another twenty to thirty years and doing a great deal more of his splendid work."

"You have heard of Papa?" Larentia asked.

"I cannot pretend that I have read many of his books," Mr. Curtis answered, "but I am aware in what estimation he is held by those who are interested in mediaeval history."

"I hope you will tell Papa so," Larentia said. "He sometimes grows despondent and feels that all his work is ignored."

"It will never be that," Mr. Curtis replied. "And I will do my best to convince him of his importance as soon as he is well enough to listen."

He would have said goodbye but Larentia said:

"There is something I want to ask you."

Mr. Curtis waited.

"I have to go away .. for a few days .. perhaps it will be .. more. Can you make some .. excuse so that Papa does not .. worry .. or even feel curious as to why I am not .. at his bed-side?"

"Yes, of course," Mr. Curtis said. "It will in fact be quite easy for me to say I have kept you away because you have a cold. I never allow my patients to come in contact with any sort of infection."

"Thank you very much," Larentia said. "I will return as soon as it is possible."

"I am sure you will, Miss Braintree, and now try not to worry. Have faith in me and in your father's will to live."

"I will do that," she answered.

She gave Mr. Curtis a brave little smile and he thought he had never seen a more beautiful girl or one who behaved so admirably in a manner which commanded his approval.

He disliked relatives who wept and sobbed and, in consequence, upset his patients who had to undergo operations.

Before she had gone to the Nursing Home Larentia had asked Harry Carrington if she could speak to Katie King.

"I think it would be a mistake," he said, "and to tell you the truth, Miss Braintree, I have not yet told Katie that you intend to impersonate her and try to obtain the money we need so desperately. I thought it might upset her."

"I understand," Larentia said, "but perhaps when it is all over I shall have the pleasure of meeting Miss King and telling her how difficult I found it to play a part that she could have done so much better."

Harry Carrington did not tell Larentia that Katie had said before he had even thought of it :

"Better not let the Braintree girl meet me."

"Why not?" Harry had enquired.

"I'm not a fool, Harry," Katie answered. "You tell me she's a lady, so all she's got to be is herself. If she's trying to act common, she'll make a mess of it. You know that as well as I do."

"You're very wise, my Katie," Harry said, and kissed the top of her small nose.

It was Katie who had helped him compose the letter in which the Duke was supposed to have said how much he wanted a son and what he would do for the woman who gave him one.

"No! He didn't talk like that, Harry," Katie said a dozen times. "Ever so smarmy he was when he thought he could get anything out of it, but underneath he was as hard as nails. He was a two-headed eagle, and don't you forget it!"

"We have to make the letter sound convincing," Harry said. "And no-one could fault the hand-writing. Thank God you kept all those cards!"

"I only hope Bodger's as good as you crack him up to be."

"He's the best forger outside Wormwood Scrubs," Harry replied, "and I swear this Marriage Certificate will pass anywhere."

"Did you get the wedding recorded in the Church?"

"Of course I did!" Harry answered. "And where do you think we chose to have His Grace hand-cuffed in Holy Matrimony?"

"I've no idea."

"Southwark Cathedral!"

Katie laughed.

"Nothing but the best!"

"That's what I thought the Duke would want, and the Bishop has been dead for three years, so there's no way of knowing whether he did or didn't marry you quietly without anybody else knowing about it!"

"How did you get into the Cathedral and find the Register?"

"Bodger broke into the Vestry and found it where we thought it would be. We filled in the names and – Bob's your uncle! Who's likely to query it?"

"No-one, I hope," Katie said quickly.

She was very critical, but she had to admit that the letter supposedly written by the Duke sounded very much like him, and his signature, which had been copied from the cards that he had sent her with the bouquets of flowers which had been the envy of all the girls in the dressing-room, was absolutely identical.

"It will convince Isaac Levy, and he will pay up," Harry said.

"I must say," Katie remarked, "he's been a sport in taking a chance on our pulling it off."

"He'll get his 'pound of flesh' all right," Harry answered dryly. "There's not going to be much left after he's had his pickings."

"There'll be enough when I can get back to the Theatre," Katie cried. "I know – I know it in my bones, Harry, that I'm going to have my name in gas-lights over the Gaiety door, just like you promised me."

She had been at first incredulous when Harry had to confess to her that without the operation she had not a chance of living, but with Larentia Braintree's help they would get the money from the Duke's family, and she would live.

"You're really going to say that he married me?" she asked.

At first the comic side of it had not struck her, then, when it did, she laughed until the tears came into her eyes.

"Can you see him, the stuck-up old Devil, marrying a common chorus-girl, or rather a ballet-dancer with a three-minute solo?"

"Who knows, if you had given him a son he might have done," Harry said.

"I suppose so," Katie answered. "Funny old world, ain't it? Think of all the trouble I've taken not to have one with you."

"God forbid!" Harry ejaculated. "Two mouths to feed is bad enough and I'm damned if I'd spend my time at home nursing the baby while you're swinging your legs in the Strand!"

Katie laughed again at the idea, and so did Harry.

Then they sat down seriously to compile a list of things Larentia had to know when she was pretending to be a Gaiety girl.

"We don't need to be too fussy," Katie said. "After all, the Garons, especially the Marchioness, are not going to know what it's like behind stage of a Music Hall."

"It's not the sort of place she would be likely to visit at any time," Harry agreed.

"Nevertheless the girl'll have to know what she's talking about."

Harry knew she was right.

He wrote down in his slightly flamboyant, but educated, hand-writing the things Larentia was to remember, then begged her to destroy the list as soon as she had learned it off by heart.

"You don't want to leave anything lying about," he said, "and remember that after the initial shock of learning who you are, they are going to try and find out how much you knew about the Duke, and doubtless about them."

"Why should they want to know that?" Larentia asked.

"Because they will want to make certain that he really married you. No man would get married without telling his wife something about his family background."

"No..I can understand..that," Larentia said.

She was so intent on getting her father into the Nursing Home and finding a plausible explanation to convince him that he could be operated on by a private Surgeon, that she did not think a great deal about herself.

Harry had come forward with the idea that an admirer of her father's who did not wish his name to be known had approached her and said he had heard of his illness through Dr. Medwin and was putting down the money for the operation anonymously.

As Harry had almost the same story to tell about Katie, Dr. Medwin was clearly incredulous.

"Now what is all this about?" he asked. "First Miss Braintree, then you, Carrington, have come up with £200 when it is the last thing I expected to happen."

"There is no reason why we should give you any explanation," Harry said, "except that we ask you to believe what Miss Braintree has told you."

"If there is any 'hokey-pokey' going on, Carrington, which will involve her in trouble, I will murder you with my own hands!" Dr. Medwin said.

"I am saving her father's life," Harry replied defiantly.

"That is not what I asked you," Dr. Medwin retorted, "and quite frankly, I am suspicious that you are up to something, though I cannot think what."

"Give me the benefit of the doubt," Harry said, "and just be thankful that two of your patients will live to bless you because you are friendly enough with Curtis to get them in quickly."

"I still cannot imagine where this money has come from," Dr. Medwin murmured.

"Perhaps one day we'll tell you," Harry replied, "but for the moment look on it as manna from Heaven and be grateful."

Unexpectedly Dr. Medwin laughed.

"I do not trust you any further than I can see you, Carrington. At the same time I have to hand it to you: there is something going on under the counter, but at least it is benefiting two worthwhile people, and I am content with that."

"Stop harassing me, Doctor!" Harry cried.

At the same time he was smiling.

* * *

It was only after Larentia had left her father at the Nursing Home that she thought about herself and said to Harry:

"I have suddenly thought of something."

"What is it?" Harry asked.

"I have packed everything I possess, but I know I shall look very .. shabby and out of place at Tregaron Castle."

"You will look beautiful," he said with a note of sincerity in his voice, "and if your clothes are shabby, remember the Duke has not been at all generous to you all these years while you have kept his secret, and because he is ill you've not had a penny from him this last six months."

His eyes narrowed before he added:

"Let them realise you have been hungry and cold during the winter because you could not afford the fuel! It will do them good to learn the facts of life for a change. The rich have no idea how the poor live!"

There was so much bitterness in his tone that Larentia knew it meant something personal to him.

She had often wondered what his background was, but had been too shy to ask questions.

It was obvious that he was a gentleman by birth, that he had been well educated, and that he must have once lived a very different life from the one he was leading now.

"I would like Papa to meet him and tell me what he thinks," she told herself. But she knew it would be a mistake for the Professor to come in contact with Harry Carrington until everything was over, and perhaps then she could be honest about what had occurred.

'Papa would be shocked at my acting a lie and trying to

extract money from the Duke, even if his wife was treated badly,' Larentia thought.

Then as she said a little prayer that she might be forgiven, she could only remember that whatever she was doing and however reprehensible it might be she was saving her father's life.

She loved him and he must live, nothing else was of any consequence.

Chapter Three

The servants withdrew and the Dowager Marchioness of Humber was left alone with her nephew, the 5th Duke of Tregaron.

They appeared to be sitting in a small lighted island in the middle of the huge Dining-Room that could easily hold a hundred people, and it had already come to the new Duke's mind that in future, except when there was a party, he would dine in what had once been called the Private Dining-Room.

But now the great pointed Gothic ceiling with its carved stone capitals seemed full of dark shadows, while the candles on the table glittered on the gold ornaments which were part of the history of the Garon family.

"You must be tired, Aunt Muriel," the Duke said, as the Marchioness sipped her coffee.

"I am a little," she confessed, "and if you will excuse me, Justin, I will go to bed as soon as we have finished dinner. It has been an exhausting three days having so many people in the house."

The Duke smiled a little cynically.

"I could not help being amused by the number of the family who turned up to pay their respects to Uncle Murdoch when he was dead, when none of them had a good word to say for him when he was alive."

"And not without reason," the Marchioness replied. "You were told his last words were that you would make a better Duke than he has been, and that is what we expect of you, Justin. It should not be difficult."

"I never expected to inherit," the Duke replied. "In

fact, I was sure that with three wives and his women following one after the other, Uncle Murdoch sooner or later would produce a son or have one foisted on him."

"That is what we have always been afraid of," the Marchioness said frankly.

There was a note in her voice which told the Duke it had been a very real fear.

Then she said briskly:

"What you have to do now, Justin, is to settle down and have a large family. It has been a tradition of the Garons for hundreds of years, and it always puzzled me why my brother was unable to produce a son."

Justin could not make the obvious reply and after a moment he said:

"Before I think of marriage there are a great many things to be done. The estate, I am quite certain, needs new ideas and perhaps new people to administer it, and I cannot help feeling that with Uncle Murdoch oblivious to what has been going on there has been a great deal of unnecessary extravagance or perhaps even thieving."

"I am sure you will prove yourself to be a very good organiser," the Marchioness said, "and that reminds me, I think it is time you retired the Chaplain and replaced him with a younger man."

"I have already thought that myself."

He met his aunt's eyes and they were both thinking that the Chaplain, who had had an easy time of it for so many years, had relieved his boredom in drink.

They were also aware that the services which should have taken place regularly in the private Chapel for the staff and anyone else on the estate who wished to attend, had been reduced to only one a month.

The Duke started thinking of that and many other things that required his attention.

It was true that he had never expected to inherit the Dukedom, nor had he thought it at all likely that his uncle would die at such a comparatively early age.

The Garons had a tradition of longevity and he had been sensible enough not to waste his time waiting for 'dead men's shoes'.

He had, instead, filled his life with the activities at which he excelled, and this had led to some interesting experiences arising from his exceptional ability to speak several languages besides his own.

He had travelled frequently to far off parts of the world at other people's expense, and he wondered now if he would find what his aunt called 'settling down' rather dull after the many adventures which had come his way in the last few years.

Then he told himself that besides his responsibility for and the reorganisation of the Garon estates, he would also find a place waiting for him in the House of Lords. Politics had always been something which interested him, especially when they concerned Foreign Affairs.

The Marchioness finished her coffee and put down her cup.

"I will leave you to your port, Justin," she said, "and tomorrow I must make plans for returning home."

"Do not hurry to do so, Aunt Muriel," the Duke replied. "You know I like having you here and your advice on family matters has been of tremendous value to me. After all, I have been out of touch for a number of years."

"There are plenty of other relatives eager to tell you anything you want to know," the Marchioness said with a smile, "but you know I am always there if you want me. In fact, I am flattered that you should do so."

She rose as she spoke and the Duke crossed the room ahead of her to open the door.

The Marchioness paused beside it.

"Good-night, dear boy," she said. "It makes me very happy to see you in my father's place. He was a fine man and I am sure that he would be very proud of his grandson."

"Thank you," the Duke said simply.

He bent as he spoke and kissed his aunt's cheek, then walking with her head high and her back stiff in her usual regal fashion the Marchioness started down the corridor towards the Great Hall.

The Duke went back to his place at the head of the table and poured himself a very small glass of port from the cut-glass decanter.

He took it in his hand and looked up to where over the stone mantelpiece there was a picture of one of the first Garons to live in the Castle, Sir Justin Garon, after whom he was named.

"To the Garons!" he said. "And may I be worthy of you, Sir Justin, and all those who followed you to embellish our name in the history of England!"

He drank his port, then sat back in his chair, a smile of amusement on his lips.

He had felt very conscious of the Castle's magnificence when he had come home, and of the part it had played in shaping his character when he was a small boy.

Because he had disliked his uncle and his appalling reputation he had, as soon as he was old enough to know his own mind, never stayed in the Castle.

He had, however, spent a great deal of time there as a child because his father loved it and his grandfather liked having his family permanently around him.

Yet although he no longer said it, it had always been in his mind, and he knew that when he dreamed at night it was not of a woman but of the turrets and towers that were imbued with a spiritual quality that he could never find in any female.

He was just thinking that he would leave the Dining-Room when the door opened and the Butler came towards him.

"Excuse me, Your Grace. There's a young lady here asking for Her Ladyship, but as she's retired to bed I don't like to disturb her."

"No, of course not, Dalton," the Duke replied. "But

surely it is rather late for anybody to be calling?"

"I don't think it is a social call, M'Lord. The young lady, as I understand it, has come from London specially to see Her Ladyship on a private matter."

"From London, at this hour of the night?"

"Yes, M'Lord, and she's very insistent that she must speak to Her Ladyship, and I don't think she will go away until she has done so."

The Duke was just about to say that his uncle's Secretary and Comptroller who had run the Castle for years could see the caller, when he remembered that he had sent Mr. Arran to London immediately after the Funeral.

This was because following the announcement of the Duke's death there would inevitably be demands for money and perhaps even suggestions of blackmail from the women with whom the late Duke had associated indiscriminately.

To himself Justin described them as the 'sweepings of Piccadilly', and he was quite certain that they would do everything in their power to extort money from the estate now that the man who had spent so much on them, for so many years, had gone to his grave.

"We must have no scandals, Arran," he said. "At the same time, if we are over-generous with one, the next day there will be a dozen to take her place."

"I am well aware of that, Your Grace," Mr. Arran replied, "and I have been horrified these past years, to know how much money has been expended on such trash!"

"It is something which will not occur in the future," the Duke said and his voice was hard.

Now, unfortunately, Arran was not there to cope in a way in which he was undoubtedly expert, and the Duke said with a touch of irritation in his voice:

"I presume I shall have to see this woman. I suppose she has a conveyance to take her away when I have finished with her?"

The Butler looked embarrassed.

"I'm afraid not, M'Lord."

He saw the question in the Duke's eyes and explained quickly:

"I was having my supper downstairs, M'Lord, and there was only a footman on duty. She came here in a hackney-carriage from the station and the coachman had unloaded her trunk and driven away without James insisting he should wait."

The Duke's lips tightened.

It was really an intolerable imposition, he thought, for somebody to arrive so late and automatically expect to be housed.

"Where have you put this importunate visitor?" he asked rising to his feet.

"I have shown her into the Writing-Room, M'Lord, being the nearest room to the front door. Would Your Lordship prefer to see her elsewhere?"

"Yes, in the Library," the Duke answered.

He left the Dining-Room and proceeded down the corridor towards the Library which was on the other side of the Great Hall.

He thought how annoying it was when he had looked forward to a quiet evening, thinking over his plans for the future, that he should be interrupted by a stranger, who had doubtless come to ask for money.

His uncle's acquaintances of the female sex were not interested in anything else.

It would doubtless be a hard-luck story, and the woman had been astute enough to ask for the Marchioness because his aunt was known for her good works and her generosity to a number of charities, which also had the blessing of the Queen.

"She will find I am not so soft," the Duke told himself.

When he entered the huge Library which was one of the features of the Castle he stood with his back to the carved mediaeval fireplace with its brilliantly painted heraldic coat-of-arms.

58

The books which had been accumulated over the centuries stretched from floor to ceiling, and there was a balcony on one side of the Library which could be reached by a small twisting stairway which the Duke remembered he had found an exciting plaything when he was a child.

Now he thought with satisfaction that he would have room to house his own collection of books which was smaller than he would have wished merely because he was continually on the move.

The door opened and the Butler announced:

"Miss Katie King, M'Lord!"

The Duke watched a slight figure come into the room.

For a moment, as she was beyond the light of the oil-lamps, he could only see that she was wearing a long, dark cloak and she moved towards him very slowly as if she was nervous.

Then as she drew nearer he saw a thin face with a small pointed chin dominated by two very large eyes that were looking at him apprehensively.

It flashed through his mind that she was unexpectedly lovely, then beneath the small plain bonnet trimmed with cheap ribbons he saw her hair and drew in his breath.

At first he thought he must be imagining the colour of it, then secondly that it must be dyed.

Then as she stood looking up at him he knew, incredibly, unbelievably, that he was seeing hair the colour of the Goddess Diana's, that he had last looked at in the *Comte's* house in Paris.

Because he did not speak the woman facing him seemed to feel she must say something, and in a voice that was soft, musical and at the same time nervous she said quickly:

"I .. I must apologise for .. arriving so .. I. late .. but the train was d. delayed .. and I did not .. know where else I could .. go."

Larentia knew she could not explain to this overwhelming man that she had found to her consternation that she did not have enough money to stay at an Inn, even if there had been one available.

The station to which Harry Carrington had sent her, which he had told her was only six or seven miles from the Castle, was situated in what appeared to be only a small village and it had, in fact, been difficult to hire a carriage to bring her to the Castle.

When Larentia had started her journey and had travelled for some way in the second class compartment where Harry Carrington had put her she found that her ticket would only take her to her destination and he had not bought her a 'return'.

She had the feeling, although it might be unjust, that he was deliberately making sure that she would strive in every way she could to obtain the money they needed.

It also frightened her to realise that she had not only no return fare, but very little other money to expend on anything she required.

She had no idea what it would cost for a carriage to take her the six or seven miles from the station to the Castle, and although the country Inn might be cheap, she could not imagine what it would be like.

She was really afraid to stay in an Inn even if they would accept, which she thought might be unlikely, a woman travelling alone.

She was aware how horrified her father would be of her making the journey in the first place, and the idea of her hiring a room in a public place where men of every class could buy drinks, was something he would not have contemplated, even for one instant.

She had therefore, late though it was, known that she must come on to the Castle and hope that the Marchioness would be kind enough to let her stay the night.

It was when they arrived that the cabman, instead of waiting as Larentia hoped he would, in case the Marchioness would not see her, had said in a surly tone:

'Oi got t'get back!'"

"Will you please wait for a few minutes?" Larentia enquired.

He had shaken his head.

"Oi wants me money."

Because she felt it was uncomfortable to make a scene in front of the footman, she had paid him and he dumped her small trunk down on the step for the flunkey to carry inside.

Then he had driven off without even thanking her for the tip she gave him.

This had made her even more nervous than she was already and now when the Duke did not speak, she felt she must explain her presence before her voice died on her, from sheer fright.

"The trains are often late in this part of the world," the Duke said at length, "but anyway my aunt has retired for the night, so perhaps you will tell me why you are so anxious to see her."

It was the last thing she wanted to do, Larentia thought.

She had planned all the way on her journey to the Castle what she would say to the Marchioness, thinking that an elderly lady would be sympathetic towards a secret marriage.

Harry Carrington had found out a great deal about the Marchioness.

He had discovered from reference books which he found in the Public Library, how many Charities she sponsored, and told Larentia that he also had friends who had spoken of her generosity, and said that she was sympathetic to the work the Prime Minister, Mr. Gladstone, was doing amongst 'fallen women'.

For a moment Larentia had not known what he meant by the expression. Then, as a suspicion of what it might be came to her mind, the colour deepened in her cheeks.

"I'm not suggesting for a moment," Harry had said quickly, "that that is what you are pretending to be. The Duke married Katie because she was good and wouldn't accept any other position in his life save that of his wife. I am only explaining to you how understanding the Marchioness is likely to be."

"Yes .. yes .. of course," Larentia had said, feeling this was a very embarrassing conversation to be having with a man.

It had never struck her for one moment that she might not be able to talk to the Marchioness, but would be confronted instead by the Duke.

He was so tall and he seemed, even in the most enormous Castle she had ever imagined, to be overpowering, and, in fact, terrifying.

Also the way he was looking at her made her feel that he penetrated her disguise and knew in fact that she was not Katie King or the Duchess of Tregaron, but just the daughter of an impoverished Professor.

Then she reminded herself that it was not her own fears that mattered. At this very moment her father and Katie were having their lives saved because money had been paid for their operations.

This had only been lent on the supposition that she would be clever enough to extract it from the Garon family.

She had disliked Mr. Isaac Levy whom Harry Carrington had brought to meet her one afternoon when her father was asleep.

He was an elderly man with a large hooked nose and greasy black hair, and he stared at her with his dark eyes in a way that made her feel uncomfortable.

She thought he was inspecting her as a man might inspect a race-horse on which he is going to stake his money in a race, and he then had rubbed his long thin fingers together.

Although he had said nothing she had known by the expression on Harry's face that Isaac Levy would lend them the money and her father's life would be saved.

Even so it had been difficult to thank him and even more difficult to shake his hand before he left.

When he had gone she told herself that whatever Mr. Levy loaned them must be returned because she could not bear to be under an obligation to him.

Now as if the Duke was suddenly aware that she was standing waiting for him to speak, he said:

"Will you sit down, Miss King? And perhaps after such a long journey you would care for some refreshment. May I offer you a glass of wine?"

"No .. thank you," Larentia answered. "But perhaps I could have a .. a glass of water?"

It was something she needed because her lips were dry and she was in fact both hungry and thirsty.

Because she had so little money she had not dared to buy anything at the stations at which the train had stopped on the journey, and she was also nervous of going to the over-crowded, noisy bars where drinks were served to travellers besides food, which looked extremely unappetising.

"Of course you may have some water, if that is what you prefer," the Duke was saying, "but if you do not care for wine, I am sure you would like coffee."

It suddenly struck him that she looked very pale and he added:

"When did you last have something to eat? I know it is often difficult at stations to procure anything edible."

"I .. I am .. all right," Larentia said hastily.

"That is not what I asked you."

"N . nothing .. since I left .. London."

He looked at her in astonishment. Then he rang the bell which hung at the side of the mantelpiece.

The door was opened almost immediately by a footman who was on duty outside in the passage.

"You rang, M'Lord?"

"Yes. Ask the Chef to prepare something quickly for Miss King. Soup and perhaps an omelette should not take long."

"Very good, M'Lord."

As the footman shut the door, Larentia said:

63

"I am .. sorry to be such a .. nuisance. I was sure that I would .. get here much earlier in the evening .. and be able to see Her Ladyship ..."

"I hope I may take her place adequately," the Duke said dryly. "Perhaps I might suggest, Miss King, that you would be more comfortable without your cloak and your bonnet?"

He could not resist the opportunity of seeing the rest of her hair.

Although he kept looking at it, he could hardly believe that he was not being tricked into believing that it was as beautiful as it appeared to be.

Obediently, as if she was a child who had been given an order, Larentia rose and undid her cape where it fastened at the neck.

The Duke took it from her and crossed the room to lay it on a chair near the door.

When he turned back he saw that Larentia had untied the ribbons of her bonnet and taken it from her head, and now the light glinted on the gold touching it with fire.

He would have staked his fortune and his newly-inherited title that the colour was completely genuine and owed nothing to artifice.

Never had he seen such hair except in a picture, and now when he looked at Larentia again he realised she was, incredible though it seemed, a living replica of Diana as Boucher had visualised her, all those years ago.

Larentia put her bonnet down on a chair next to the one on which she was sitting, then she put her hands in her lap and stared at the Duke as if she was suddenly at a loss as to what she should do and how she was to proceed.

He wondered what could make her so nervous, and to put her at her ease sat down on the other side of the hearth.

"Now tell me, Miss King," he said, "why you have come here. It must be of importance for you to have come such a long way."

"Y . yes . . it is very important," Larentia agreed.

She knew he was waiting, but she had to force herself to open her handbag and take out the two pieces of paper it contained.

What she really wanted to do was to run away; to say it was all a terrible mistake, and go back to London to her house which was the only secure thing in her life.

Then she told herself she must not be afraid but think of her father and the pain which had contorted his handsome face even when they were on their way to the Nursing Home.

In a very small voice she said :

"I . . I have . . brought these . . for you . . to see."

She held out the two pieces of paper as she spoke towards the Duke, feeling she should perhaps rise and go over to him, but felt, if she did so, her legs would not support her.

He reached across the hearth-rug to take them from her. Then he sat back, crossing his legs and very much at his ease to open the first one.

It was the Marriage Certificate.

As he read it, Larentia felt she could not look at him, but clasped her hands, squeezing her fingers together until they hurt.

Slowly and deliberately the Duke opened the letter and read it. Then there was a silence which Larentia found unbearable until he asked :

"How old are you?"

"I am . . twenty-three . . nearly twenty-four."

Larentia had expected this question and was ready for it and the only hesitation was because she thought she had lost her voice and no sound seemed to come from her throat.

"So you were seventeen when you were married to my uncle?"

"Y . yes."

"I presume your father or mother gave permission for the marriage?"

This was another question Harry Carrington had warned her to expect.

"They were .. both dead."

"I see as you are described as 'actress' that you were earning your living on the stage."

"Yes."

"Where?"

"At the .. Olympic .. Music .. Hall."

The Duke nodded as if he had heard of it, then he looked again at the letter and the Marriage Certificate before he asked:

"Were you surprised that anyone so important as the Duke of Tregaron should wish to marry you?"

"He took me out to supper .. many times .. before he .. actually suggested it."

Harry had told her to say this and had added:

"Katie was a good girl, and as I explained to you, the Duke made a suggestion that she should occupy a very different position in his life. Of course she refused!"

"Of course," Larentia had said, and again she had blushed.

"I suppose you realise," the Duke said, after what seemed to Larentia a long pause, "that if you are as you say you are, the Duchess of Tregaron, you are, on my uncle's death, in a very advantageous position."

"I do not .. want to be a Duchess," Larentia said quickly. "Why I am here is simply because I have not .. received the .. money that he has been .. paying me these past six years, to keep our .. marriage a .. secret."

"He has been paying you?" the Duke asked, and it struck Larentia that she had told her story very badly.

Harry had explained to her exactly what she must say, but because she had been so frightened by the lateness of the hour, the size of the Castle and by the Duke himself, she had really started at the wrong end of her explanation instead of at the beginning.

After drawing a deep breath she said quickly:

"What I wanted to tell you was that after we had been married and I did not..give His Grace the..son he wanted, he told me that he would give me enough money for me to be comfortable as long as I told nobody that we ..were married."

She felt her voice falter, then by sheer will-power continued:

"I..I gave him my..sacred promise which I have kept ..that I would never tell a soul what had occurred..but for the last six months the money has not come..and I need it."

"How much was it?" the Duke asked. "And how did you receive it?"

"He gave me fifteen pounds a month..and it came by post."

"Is that all?"

"Yes..it was quite enough..especially as I was.. working."

"Where are you acting now?"

"I was at the Gaiety until two months ago when I fell ill. I had a..fever that would not go away..and that is why I need the money..so badly..as I was not earning anything."

"Of course, I understand that," the Duke said, "and when you learnt that the Duke was dead you realised there would be no more money unless the family provided it."

"That is..what I..hoped you would do," Larentia answered, "and I..promise to go on keeping the secret for..ever if you will be kind enough not to give it to me by the month, but as a lump sum..that would..last me for the..rest of my life."

Harry's words in which he had rehearsed her, seemed to tumble out a little incoherently, but they were said, and now for a moment she felt as if the room swung around her and she felt dizzy.

The Duke spoke again, but she could not hear what he said. He seemed to have gone very far away. Then she was aware that he was speaking to somebody, but it was too difficult to think of him or even to understand the words he was saying.

The next thing Larentia knew was that somebody was holding a glass to her lips.

"Take a sip!" a voice ordered and she obeyed.

"And another!"

She thought it was not water she was drinking, but something very much stronger. Then as she felt almost as if there was something fiery running down her throat, she opened her eyes and realised that the Duke was bending over her.

"I .. I am .. sorry," she tried to say.

"Drink a little more," he suggested, but she shook her head.

"I am .. all right .. please .. forgive me."

"Where is the food? It is taking a long time!"

The Duke was not speaking to her but to the man who was standing behind him, the Butler, who was holding a tray on which there was a decanter.

"I will see to it, Your Grace."

"Tell them to bring the soup. That could not take so long."

"Yes, Your Grace."

With her head against a silk cushion Larentia thought she should sit upright but it was too much effort to move.

The brandy which she realised she had drunk began to move away the mist before her eyes and she could think more clearly.

The Duke did not speak but only stood waiting and after a few minutes the door opened and the Butler re-appeared with two footmen behind him.

He put a small table covered by a lace cloth in front of Larentia, then set down a tray on which there was a small silver tureen and a soup-plate of such exquisite china that, weak as she was, she found herself admiring it.

There was a white linen napkin to put over her knees, and the Butler ladled the soup onto the china plate and, without asking her, filled a glass with wine.

Because she knew it would be polite when they had taken so much trouble Larentia made herself sit up and start to drink the soup.

It was clear, warm and delicious, and she found unexpectedly that she was hungry and finished what was on her plate without even looking at the Duke who was sitting watching her.

Then the footman appeared with another dish containing an omelette filled with creamy mushrooms and slightly browned on top which Larentia, who was in fact a good cook, knew meant it was done to perfection.

Again she ate without speaking, then feeling very much stronger she drank a little of the wine and without it being an effort, she managed to smile at the Duke.

"Now do you feel better?" he asked.

"I am .. ashamed of behaving in .. such a foolish manner."

"It was quite understandable," he said. "You have had a very long journey, and as you say, you have not been well."

The Butler came forward to remove the tray from the table.

"Is there anything else you would like?" the Duke asked.

"No, thank you."

The Butler and the footman walked to the door and when it had shut behind them the Duke asked:

"Do you feel strong enough to renew our conversation, or shall we leave it until tomorrow?"

"P . perhaps you would like to .. think over what I have .. said."

"I understand that you will promise to go on keeping your marriage to my uncle a secret, provided we look after you financially. You would prefer to receive a lump sum rather than be paid monthly as you have been up until now?"

"Yes.. I thought it was a better.. arrangement."

"What sum do you think would ensure your silence, presumably for the rest of your life?"

Ever since she had agreed to Harry Carrington's scheme that was the moment Larentia had felt would be the most embarrassing.

£5,000 was an incredible sum of money, and although Harry Carrington had said over and over again that it would mean nothing to the Duke, she still felt that to ask for so much seemed greedy and in her own opinion, likely to make the Garons feel that they were almost being blackmailed.

"And that is exactly what they are," she had told herself on the train. "Blackmail means that you are trying to extort money from somebody by threatening to expose them if they do not pay you! That is what I am doing, and it makes me feel like a criminal!"

Harry Carrington had been quite cross with her when she had suggested she should ask for half that amount and hope the family would give more.

"Why should they not be generous now that the Duke is dead?" he asked sharply. "Besides, have you ever known anyone who wishes to part with more money than they are compelled to? Let me tell you – it's the rich who are mean and ungenerous, except when it suits their purpose."

His voice had been sharp as he had gone on:

"If they can get away with tuppence halfpenny they will! You do as I tell you and ask for £5,000. They may screw you down, but I doubt it. They will be too frightened that you will demand everything you are entitled to as a Duchess."

Yet the fact that she now had to say what she was asking made Larentia wish that she could fade away into unconsciousness again.

"I am waiting to hear what you are asking," the Duke prompted.

"I thought .. perhaps .. £5,000," Larentia said, in a voice that was little above a whisper.

She could not look at him as she spoke but could only stare down at her hands and know that she was blushing in a way which always made her feel shy.

"You think that is a right and just sum?" the Duke asked.

"Perhaps .. you may think it .. is too much," Larentia faltered.

"If you want the truth," he replied, "I think you have been very loyal and behaved in an exemplary manner in keeping your marriage a secret for so long, but I am wondering what you will do now if I refuse to give you the money."

Larentia's head went up quickly and her eyes, as she looked at him, were wide and terrified.

"But you must give it to me!" she said. "I must have *some* of it at any rate!"

"Why is it so urgent?"

"Because I have a .. commitment which must be .. paid."

She said the first words which came into her mind and she could only think of Isaac Levy waiting for the return of his loan and what would happen if she went back empty-handed.

"A certain commitment?" the Duke repeated quietly. "You mean that you are in debt?"

"Yes .. yes .. that is it," Larentia said, "I am in debt .. and if I cannot pay what I .. owe I may have to .. take the consequences."

It was quite obvious from the expression on her face and the desperation in her voice that the consequences were frightening.

"How much is your debt exactly?" the Duke asked.

Frantically Larentia tried to do a sum in her head – £200

for each operation, and it was only just by chance that Harry Carrington had let out that Isaac Levy expected not 50 per cent interest, but 100 per cent and more if it was not paid within a month.

"Twice £400 is £800," Larentia told herself.

Then in a voice that sounded even more frightened than she had been before, she managed to say:

"I .. I .. owe over .. £800."

As she spoke she thought it would be impossible for the Duke to believe her.

How could she have spent so much money looking as she did in clothes she had made herself, and which she had worn for a long time?

There was an uncomfortable silence. Then the Duke said:

"Who sent you?"

"Nobody!"

Even as she spoke Larentia prayed that she might be forgiven for telling yet another lie.

"Who told you how much money to ask for?"

"No .. one."

She wondered how she could bear this inquisition and she felt that each answer had to be torn from her as if it was a living part of her body.

The Duke looked at her in silence. Then he said:

"As I think you must be very tired I am going to suggest that you go to bed. I want to think over what you have told me and, if you will allow me to do so, to discuss it with my aunt, the Dowager Marchioness of Humber, for whom you asked when you arrived. Then, of course, I shall have to consult my Lawyers."

"W . why?" Larentia asked. "Why should you .. wish to do that? Surely you could just .. give me the money and let me .. go back to London?"

"You are in a hurry to get back? Why?"

"I have to get back to the .. Theatre and also .. there is someone who needs me."

"A man?"

For a moment she did not understand the implication in the question, then Larentia said quickly:

"It is someone who is very ill and whom I am looking after."

"So you cannot be spared, especially as you cannot afford to pay anybody to take your place."

"Yes, that is .. right."

"I clearly understand what you want," the Duke said, "but you will appreciate that this evidence you have brought me is very serious from the point of view of the family. If you are in fact, as you say, the wife of the 4th Duke of Tregaron, then it is something which must be added to our genealogical tree, and be incorporated in the archives of the family to go down with all the other history of the Garons to posterity."

"No .. no," Larentia said quickly. "There is .. no need for that! It was a secret marriage .. and I quite understand it must remain .. secret for all time .. all I ask is that you will .. substantiate the promise the Duke gave me that I might have a little comfort .. as long as I keep my word to him."

"I hardly think he was very generous."

"That was .. all I needed at the time .. but I would like now to be .. free of the necessity of watching for the money to arrive .. and feeling that I cannot .. manage without it."

"How long do you think £5,000 would last you, and how could we be certain that when you had spent it, you would not come back for more?" the Duke asked.

"I can only give you my word."

"The word that you have kept most discreetly for six years," the Duke agreed. "Nevertheless times change, you will get older, and perhaps it will be no longer possible for you to appear on the stage. What happens then?"

"Oh .. please ..." Larentia begged. "Do not let us concern ourselves with that .. but just with the present. I need £800 desperately. In fact .. I have to have that! The rest is not so important."

She knew Harry Carrington would be furious with her. At the same time she told herself all that really mattered was that the two operations could be paid for and they were no longer in debt to Isaac Levy.

It flashed through her mind that neither her father nor Katie King might be able to earn any money for some time.

"In which case, I must earn some," Larentia told herself, and wondered helplessly what she could do.

She was aware that the Duke was watching her face and the expressions that followed one after another in her green-tinged eyes.

Then she looked at him pleadingly.

"Please .. do not make things too .. difficult for me," she said. "It has been very hard to come here .. and I only wish I could .. manage without having to beg money. It is .. humiliating .. degrading .. but there was nothing else I could do."

She sounded so pathetic that the Duke found it difficult not to be moved by her voice and the expression in her eyes and by the way the light seemed almost to dance on her hair as she moved her head.

"I have already said that you should go to bed," he replied. "In the morning things will perhaps not seem quite so upsetting as they are at the moment."

"And you .. will let me .. return to London .. as soon as possible?"

"I will keep in mind what you wish to do," he replied.

He rose as he spoke and because she felt it impossible to go on pleading with him Larentia rose too.

The Duke rang the bell.

"May I keep this letter and also your Marriage Certificate to show my aunt?" he enquired.

"Yes, of course."

He looked down at her and asked:

74

"Are you not rather trusting? Suppose I destroy them?"

It was the same question Larentia had asked Harry Carrington and she replied:

"I know you would think it very wrong to do so, and besides, if you wish, you can of course see the entry of the marriage in the Register which is kept in Southwark Cathedral."

She thought as she spoke, that Harry Carrington would have been pleased with her answer, and she had the feeling, although she could not be sure, that the Duke too thought it was a convincing one.

The door opened and the Butler asked:

"You rang, Your Grace?"

"Miss King will be staying here the night. Will you take her to Mrs. Fellows?"

"Very good, Your Grace."

The Duke put out his hand to Larentia.

"Good-night, Miss King. I hope you sleep well. I know you must be very tired after such an exhausting day."

Larentia curtsied and when her hand touched the Duke's he found it was very cold and he was aware that her fingers trembled in his.

He watched her as she walked across the room to the door, her hair arranged at the back of her head in two heavy plaits which seemed to have come from the heart of the sun.

Then as the door closed he said beneath his breath:

"Uncle Murdoch and that girl! I do not believe it!"

Chapter Four

"You are very early, Justin!" the Dowager Marchioness said as the Duke came into the Boudoir that adjoined her bedroom.

She was fully dressed. She would not have thought of receiving anyone, even her nephew, wearing a négligée.

Her lace corsets held her stiffly upright, her hair was well arranged by her maid, she wore five ropes of pearls and had several diamond rings on her blue-veined hands.

"I apologise, Aunt Muriel," the Duke replied, "but I have something of great importance to tell you, and I need your advice on what is a very urgent family matter."

The Marchioness looked at him in surprise and he seated himself in a chair beside her while her lady's maid carried away the tray which had contained her breakfast.

When the door was closed the Duke said:

"Last night, after you had left me, I was told a young woman had called asking to see you."

"To see me, so late!" the Marchioness exclaimed.

"That is exactly what I said," the Duke answered, "but as I did not wish to disturb you I saw her. She informed me that six years ago she had become the wife of Uncle Murdoch."

For a moment it seemed as if the Marchioness could not take in what the Duke had told her. Then her whole body seemed to stiffen and she said in a voice that was curiously unlike her own:

"Did you say he was – married?"

"The young woman who was, she avers, only seventeen when the wedding took place, is not the type with whom he usually associated. At the same time, she is on the stage."

The Marchioness closed her eyes for a moment, and although the Duke thought she was rather pale, she was admirably controlled as she remarked:

"An actress! I suppose that was what we might have expected!"

"Not exactly an actress," the Duke said, "but what is known in London as a Gaiety Girl."

"And Murdoch actually married her?"

"She has brought with her her Marriage Certificate and a letter from Uncle Murdoch saying that he married her because he believed she would give him a son."

"That is what I always feared," the Marchioness said in a low voice. "And did she do so?"

"Fortunately no, but apparently when she failed to produce what he wanted Uncle Murdoch paid her to keep the marriage a secret."

"And she has done so all these years?"

"Surprisingly she has kept her word," the Duke said. "She swears she has told no-one that she is the Duchess of Tregaron."

"How can you be sure of this?" the Marchioness asked. "Quite frankly, Justin, I do not believe that Murdoch, fool though he was, would have married a woman of that sort, unless he was quite certain she was carrying his child."

"The same idea certainly struck me," the Duke said. "At the same time, on the face of it, the Marriage Certificate looks valid and the letter is in Uncle Murdoch's handwriting, as you can see for yourself."

He held out the letter to the Marchioness who took it from him in a way which said all too clearly she hated even to touch anything which she felt was defiled.

She opened her lorgnette which she wore hanging from her neck on a gold chain interspersed with pearls and read the letter slowly.

Then she handed it back to the Duke as if she was glad to be rid of it, saying:

"You let this woman stay here in the house last night?"

"There was nowhere else she could go."

"Nevertheless I think it was a mistake. It might appear as if we had accepted her story."

"Perhaps that is what we will have to do."

"I do not believe for one moment that this creature is really the Duchess of Tregaron!"

"That remains to be proved," the Duke said, "but I do not think we shall do any good by antagonising her."

"What else do you expect us to do?" the Marchioness asked fiercely. "How can we contemplate for a moment, that a common woman who walks the stage for anyone who pays to look at her, should bear our name and be accepted as my brother's legal wife?"

She shut her eyes again as if at the horror of the idea.

Then she said:

"All down the centuries there have been male relatives who have misconducted themselves in one way or another. There have been Rakes, Rogues and Roués! But the Garon women have always had dignity and blue blood has flowed in their veins of which no succeeding generation need be ashamed."

"I am aware of that, Aunt Muriel," the Duke said, "but this is a problem, and you and I have to solve it."

"How can we do that?"

"What this girl has asked, and incidentally her name is Katie King, is that we give her a lump sum of £5,000 and she will continue the silence she has kept for six years for the rest of her life."

"One could hardly accept the word of a woman like that," the Marchioness said scathingly.

"She sounded convincing," the Duke replied reflectively, "in that she does not wish to be acknowledged as a Duchess and is more vitally concerned in paying a debt she owes of £800."

"In which case, why is she asking for £5,000?"

"I cannot help thinking," the Duke replied, "that some-body has suggested that sum to her, and I feel sure there is a sharp brain behind the whole exercise."

"Do you mean that somebody is trying to blackmail us into providing the money?"

"I naturally assumed that is so," the Duke answered, but we must have evidence to prove such a contention. In the meantime the woman is here and I am not quite certain what we should do about her."

"I refuse, I absolutely refuse to associate in any way with the type of woman that your uncle was seen with in London, and whom he actually entertained in Garon House."

The Marchioness drew in her breath before she added:

"I have never mentioned this to you before, but I have heard of the orgies that took place in what was always our London home! It was at Garon House that I had my coming out Ball which was attended by the Queen herself, and from Garon House I was married. Your uncle made it nothing more than a pig-sty!"

The way she spoke was so vehement that the Duke was surprised.

He had always realised the Marchioness deeply resented anything that damaged or defamed the family name.

She was in other ways such a warm-hearted, kindly woman that it almost shocked him to hear her speaking in such a bitter, violent manner against her own brother.

Yet he could understand only too well what she was feeling, and he knew far better than she did to what depths of depravity the late Duke had sunk and the vices with which he had amused himself.

Now the Duke said quietly:

"You will find Miss King is very different from the sort of woman you are visualising her to be, and we must re-member that she was only seventeen when she married Uncle Murdoch. I gather he left her very shortly after the wedding."

"She could only have married him for his title and his money."

"I suppose so," the Duke admitted, "but she does not wish to use the title, and he has certainly not been over-generous to her in the six years they have been apart."

"What did he give her?"

The Duke told her, and as he expected the Marchioness looked surprised.

"Is that all?"

"All she admits to."

"She must have been aware that Murdoch was an ex-ceedingly rich man."

"She says she does not wish to capitalise on that and has only come here now because she has been ill. Unable to earn any money herself she is heavily in debt."

"It sounds a very familiar story to me," the Marchioness said. "These women will lie and lie and no-one except the Prime Minister would believe their 'hard luck' stories, which are invented to wring the hearts of those who listen to them."

The Duke was surprised at the hardness in his aunt's voice, and it struck him that the great ladies who sat on Charity Committees were always ready to be generous to the poor and needy, except when it concerned them personally.

At the same time, he could understand what a shock it had been to the Marchioness to learn that her brother was married and to a woman whose profession would scan-dalise the whole family when they learned of it.

This thought made him say aloud:

"What I am going to suggest to you, Aunt Muriel, is that you should meet this young woman and give me your advice on what we should do about her for the moment."

He saw the expression in the Marchioness's eyes and went on quickly:

"I have as it happens already sent a letter to Arran in London explaining the circumstances and asking him to make discreet enquiries about a Gaiety Girl called Katie King, and also of course to check if the marriage is entered in the Register at Southwark Cathedral."

"Did you say they were married at Southwark Cathedral?" the Marchioness asked.

"That is what it says on the Marriage Certificate," the Duke replied. "See for yourself."

He handed his aunt the Certificate. She looked at it then said:

"This convinces me more than anything else could that her story is untrue."

"Why?"

"Because your uncle quarrelled with most of the Clergy but especially with the Bishop of Southwark."

The Marchioness thought for a moment, then she said:

"It must have been eight, perhaps ten years ago when Her Majesty was distressed by some unpleasant and sensational reports of your uncle's behaviour which appeared in the cheaper newspapers."

She gave a little sigh as if it hurt her to think of it before she continued:

"I do not know who brought it to Her Majesty's notice, but she spoke to me about it and I could only tell her how deeply distressed we were as a family at Murdoch's behaviour.

" 'I presume you can do nothing to prevent him from defaming his own name and bringing the whole of Society into disrepute?' Her Majesty asked.

" 'I am afraid not, Ma'am,' I replied. 'My brother will not listen to me, nor to anyone else.'

" 'We cannot be sure of that until we try,' the Queen replied. "I will speak to Dr. Goodwin, the Bishop of Southwark, and see if he can in any way bring the Duke to his senses.' "

The Marchioness stopped speaking and the Duke enquired:

"What happened?"

"The Bishop who was a fine man but very unworldly approached your uncle and, we presumed, remonstrated with him."

A faint smile appeared on the Duke's lips as he anticipated the end of the story.

"Apparently," the Marchioness went on, "your uncle raged at him, told him what he could do with his advice, and practically threw him out of Garon House!"

There was a pause, then the Duke said:

"So in the circumstances you think it is very unlikely that he would have married Uncle Murdoch."

"He is the last person that your uncle would have asked to do so, and I am certain after what occurred that the Bishop would have refused such a request," the Marchioness replied.

"I see your point," the Duke said.

"The Certificate certainly looks genuine enough," the Marchioness remarked, "but I suppose if there are people who can forge bank-notes they can also forge Marriage Certificates."

"This is certainly something which Arran or the detective he employs should look into," the Duke decided. "But we get back to the same question, Aunt Muriel, what are we going to do now about Miss King?"

There was an uncomfortable pause before the Marchioness said:

"I suppose I shall have to see her! I can only tell you, Justin, that I am appalled by her effrontery in coming here and forcing herself upon us, but I cannot help thinking we should be wiser to let her be dealt with by our Lawyers."

"For the time being," the Duke replied, "I think it is important that as few people as possible should know of this unfortunate claim. If the Press got hold of it Heaven knows what might appear, and as Uncle Murdoch is now dead, my desire is that he should rest in peace."

"Yes, of course," the Marchioness agreed. "That is what we all want and it is always a mistake to stir dirty water."

"That is why I think we should not antagonise Katie King. Investigations into the truth of her story will start immediately Arran receives my letter. In the meantime we must accept Miss King for what she says she is – the Duchess of Tregaron, who does not wish her identity to be known."

The Marchioness gave a little cry.

"I cannot – I will not accept her! Never! Never! My father would turn in his grave at the idea!"

"I think we must still face facts," the Duke said firmly. "The evidence Katie King has brought with her is, superficially at any rate, very convincing."

There was silence, then the Marchioness said in a stifled voice:

"Where is this creature?"

"I have no idea," the Duke replied. "I have been out riding and after I had breakfast in my own Sitting-Room I came straight to see you."

"Then send for her," the Marchioness said, "and we will see her in the Morning-Room."

"Very good, Aunt Muriel," the Duke replied, rising to his feet. "I will send a servant to tell her to be there within ten minutes."

He went from the Boudoir as he spoke and the Marchioness put her hand up to her forehead as if she sought a calmness she was far from feeling.

* * *

Larentia had felt she was living in a dream-world from the moment she had awoken to find herself in one of the loveliest bedrooms she had ever seen.

She had lain for a little while looking in the half-light at the furniture, the pictures and the carved and gilded foot of her bed.

Then she got out to run to the window.

Last night when she had first seen the Castle, she had been too nervous and agitated by what lay ahead really to take in anything except that it was enormous, far bigger than she expected, and also surprisingly beautiful.

She had arrived so late that the stars were out and there was a moon in the sky, and by its light the castellated towers of the Castle seemed to be touched with silver.

The arrow-slit windows in the whole length and breadth of it made her feel as if it was part of a fairy-tale story that had no reality.

She was aware, as her father had told her often enough, that many of the finest Castles in the whole country had been built in mediaeval times to keep the aggressive Welsh nation within their own borders.

Garon Castle was finally completed by Edward II in the early 14th century, and at the time it had been considered one of the finest Castles ever to be built in the Middle Ages.

The interior had been altered, improved and renovated over the centuries that passed, but at first sight Garon Castle had looked exactly as it had when as a Military headquarters it must certainly have awed, if not frightened, its enemies.

But to Larentia it was as if unexpectedly she had come to Camelot.

In the course of her father's work on the legends of King Arthur she had read extensively with him and sometimes for him the books and treatises he had written about the legendary sovereign.

To please him she had pored over the *Historia Britonum* of Nennius, a 9th century compilation culminating in the victory of Mt. Badon. She studied the *Annales Cambriae* and was thrilled with all the splendour and glory that Tennyson had brought to the '*Idylls of the King*'.

To her King Arthur lived and breathed as did his Knights of the Round Table, the heroic deeds they performed and the noble chivalry of their quests.

But when she had entered the Castle and been confronted by the Duke she could think only that she might be exposed.

Her terror of being sent back to London empty-handed had swept everything else from her mind, and her awe of the Duke himself as Inquisitor and Judge of the tale she had to tell left no room for fantasies.

But this morning she could think only that she was in a magical Castle and from the windows of her bedroom she could see a mystical world.

The Castle was built on a hill, and beneath it was a lake across which she could see mountains silhouetted against a blue sky.

It was to Larentia both beautiful and mystical, so that once again she was dreaming of Knights in armour dedicated to fight or die for their King and their God.

She was still standing at the window when there was a knock on the door and a maid came to call her.

"Ye're early, Miss," she said when Larentia turned to smile at her.

"The view from this window is so beautiful and I have never been in a Castle before."

"Ye'll not find a finer," the maid replied.

"That I can well believe!" Larentia said, "and I hope I shall be allowed to look over it."

"All our visitors want t'do that, Miss, an' if His Grace doesn't show ye round, Mr. Webster, the Curator'll tell ye the history of th' Barbican towers, th' Keep and th' Royal Tower. An' of course ye'll want to see th' Baron's Hall where those who fought would gather before they goes into battle."

The maid spoke in a way which made Larentia feel infected by her enthusiasm.

"I can see you love the Castle," she said softly.

"I've lived here all m' life, Miss, and m' father an' grandfather have served the Garons ever since they were small boys."

Larentia told herself she must see everything she could before she returned to London.

She dressed hurriedly and was told that her breakfast would be served to her downstairs and a footman would tell her where to go.

She felt a little shy in case the Duke would be breakfasting with her, but there was no sign of him but only the elderly Butler to enquire what she would wish to eat while a footman waited on her.

When she had finished Larentia asked if she could see a little of the Castle, unless of course the Duke had sent for her.

"His Grace is out riding, Miss, but I'm sure Mr. Webster will show you some of the Castle while you are waiting for His Grace's return."

Mr. Webster was an elderly man with white hair who had so obviously a great knowledge of history that Larentia longed to tell him who she was.

She was certain he would have heard of her father and all the time she was being taken round the rooms inside the Castle, and when she stood in the Keep where the animals and their owners were sheltered and protected when there was a battle, she kept wishing her father was with her.

She knew how much he would have enjoyed seeing the ancient Chapel which had been desecrated by the Round-heads and later restored to the way it had looked when it was erected in 1350.

She was entranced by the Armoury with its ancient weapons and heavy armour, and knew her father would have been thrilled by the portraits of each successive generation of Garons, depicting many of them wearing shining breast-plates and with a battle taking place in the background.

It was all so entrancing that Larentia had almost forgotten why she was in the Castle and the difficulties of her position when a footman came to her side to say:

"His Grace requests, Miss, that you meet him in the Morning-Room. I will take you there, if you wish."

It was almost, Larentia thought, like having a jug of cold water thrown in her face to be brought back to reality.

"Thank you, thank you," she said to the Curator. "It

has been more exciting than I can possibly tell you, to see this wonderful Castle filled with such fine treasures, and for you to tell me about it."

"It has been a pleasure, Miss King," the Curator replied, "and there is no need for me to tell you that there is a great deal more to see."

"I hope you will show it to me," Larentia replied.

Because she did not wish to keep the Duke waiting, she followed the footman quickly down the long stone passages with their Gothic-shaped doorways back to the Great Hall.

A footman opened the door of the Morning-Room and when she entered, it was with a sense of relief that she found the Duke was not present and that she had not kept him waiting.

It was a very attractive room with more portraits of the Garon family hanging on the silk-covered walls and heraldic shields portrayed on carved bosses of the mahogany ceiling.

Because she was too nervous to sit down, Larentia remained standing. Then seeing some books arranged on a round table in the window she found that among them was the latest volume published by Alfred Tennyson: 'The Holy Grail and Other Poems'.

Because she had wanted so much to read it, she picked it up and opened it.

Instinctively she was once again swept away into the world in which her father lived and breathed and which for them both was Camelot.

She was just reading:

"At once I saw him far on the great Sea
In silver-shining armour starry clear ..."[2]

– when the door opened and the Duke came into the room.

As her eyes were still bemused with what she had seen with the Curator and what she had just read she thought for one moment that he was in fact clad in silver-shining armour.

He was not a modern man but a Knight of the Round Table dedicated to defeating evil and proclaiming good.

Because for a few seconds she could not make herself step out of the past and into the present, she just stood looking at him, the book in her hand.

The sunlight pouring in from the window behind her turned her hair into flaming gold.

It seemed as if the Duke was as bemused as she was, for he stood still just inside the door, and their eyes met across the length of the room.

How long they were both of them immobile could not be counted in time. Then the Duke moved forward and the spell was broken.

As if she had been caught doing something she should not do, Larentia put down the book.

He came to her side to look down at what she had been reading and said:

"I see you have discovered Tennyson's latest poems! You like what he writes?"

"Y . yes .. Your Grace."

"Have you read any of his other works?"

"But of course! *The Idylls of the King* was based on what my father..."

Larentia stopped quickly.

She was suddenly aware that she had as the Duke approached her forgotten that she was supposed to be Katie King.

"You were speaking about your father," the Duke prompted.

"Yes, but it was not .. particularly interesting."

"I should be interested, especially if it concerns King Arthur and his Knights."

"Why do you say .. that?"

"Because here at the Castle I always feel that I am inspired by the Arthurian myths and legends and personally I like to believe that contrary to the opinion of many scholars, Arthur actually did exist."

Larentia clasped her hands together.

"But of course he did!" she exclaimed. "How can anybody doubt it when his victories in battle are described so vividly in many of the compilations? How can anybody not believe the early Welsh literature which makes him into a King of wonders and marvels?"

Only as she finished speaking, putting forward the arguments she had heard so often from her father and his friends, did she realise the Duke was looking at her with astonishment in his eyes.

"How can you be so well informed?" he asked. "Or did Mr. Webster tell you this when you were going round the Castle with him just now?"

"Actually we did not talk about King Arthur," Larentia replied, "but I have read about him ever since I was a child."

"What particular books?" the Duke asked.

Again without thinking, because the whole subject was so familiar to her, Larentia replied:

"*Mirabilia*, and of course Monmouth's *Historia regum Britanniae*."

As she looked up again at the Duke and saw the expression on his face, she thought that his astonishment was almost insulting.

There was no reason, she told herself, why he should think that she or even Katie King should be an ignoramus.

Larentia actually knew very few girls of her own age, and it had never struck her that it was very unlikely that anyone except her father's daughter would be so familiar with not only mediaeval history but also manuscripts that were only of interest to scholars.

The whole story was to her fascinating and the ancient writings as easy to read as the fairy-stories that most children had in their Nursery. But to the Duke just her appearance had taken his breath away, and now the way she was speaking made him feel utterly and completely bewildered.

"I must be dreaming," he told himself.

He knew that even more than she had done last night Larentia personified the Goddess Diana and he felt as if she had stepped out of a picture or from Olympus and now stood beside him in human guise still with her divinity about her.

With an effort to become more normal he said:

"As I see how greatly Tennyson's poems interest you, Miss King, I hope you will accept them to read while you are here and if you wish to take them away with you."

"May I do that?" Larentia asked. "How very kind! I have wanted so much to read this latest book of his poems."

The way she spoke told the Duke, without words, that she had been unable to afford to buy it and he wondered why she had not asked one of her many admirers while she was on stage, to give her a copy as a gift.

Then as Larentia looked down at the book and the Duke looked at her, the door opened and the Marchioness came in.

"Oh, here you are, Aunt Muriel!" the Duke exclaimed. "May I present Miss Katie King who, as you already know, arrived late last night to see you."

Larentia curtsied. then as she looked into the Marchioness's face she thought with a sudden sinking of her heart, that here was somebody who not only disliked but also despised her.

It was something she had not expected and instantly the nervousness she had felt when she first arrived at the Castle, returned. She told herself she must be very careful what she said and not make any mistakes.

The Marchioness did not speak but merely looked at Larentia in a way that was extremely intimidating, and it was the Duke who said:

"I think we should sit down by the fire. There is a sharp wind today, even though the sun is warm."

The Marchioness did not reply, she merely walked

towards the fireplace, the Duke followed her and Larentia came behind them reluctantly.

As she sat down in a chair, she was well aware that the atmosphere had changed, and now the bearing of the Marchioness and the expression in her eyes told her that she had to face an inquisition that was likely to be an unpleasant one.

"What is your real name?"

The Marchioness seemed to shoot the question at her and because it was unexpected and Larentia was already nervous, she replied before she could stop herself:

"Larentia."

As soon as she had spoken she realised what she had said, and added quickly: "But I dance under the name of .. Katie King."

"Is King your surname?"

"Yes."

"So you think that 'Katie King' sounds better for the stage?"

The way the Marchioness uttered the two names made them sound ludicrous and Larentia merely inclined her head in acknowledgement.

"His Grace tells me you have come here purporting to be married to my brother, the late Duke of Tregaron."

"Yes .. that is .. right."

"You have brought a Marriage Certificate and a letter. Have you no other evidence that this marriage really took place?"

"I .. I do not know what other .. evidence you would want," Larentia replied.

"When two people are to become man and wife," the Marchioness said sharply, "usually a large number of letters pass between them which would substantiate their relationship."

There was silence before Larentia said:

"I thought .. that would be all .. that you would require."

"So you do have other documents at your home – and where is that? What I am asking for, is your address."

This was a question that Harry Carrington had told Larentia she might be asked, and he had said :

"You'll have to be careful. They mustn't make enquiries either at your house or at Katie's lodgings. Tell them you've been moving about and staying with friends, and have no permanent home at the moment."

Painstakingly, almost word for word, Larentia repeated what he had told her to say.

She hoped the Duke and his aunt would think that because she had been ill and was not earning any money, that she had moved into cheaper and still cheaper lodgings, until finally on the Duke of Tregaron's death she had come to the Castle because she had nowhere else to go.

Then she remembered she had said she was looking after somebody who was ill and before the Marchioness could ask the next question, the Duke said :

"Last night you told me that you wished to return to London quickly because you were nursing somebody, but you did not say who it was."

With difficulty Larentia prevented herself from saying it was her father, recalling that Katie King's father and mother were dead.

"It is .. my uncle," she said. "He is alone in the world .. as I am .. and I have to keep house for him and now he is ill, I must be there .. to l . look after him."

"I understand," the Duke said.

"What does your uncle do?" the Marchioness enquired.

"He .. is a writer."

She was unable to think of anything but the truth.

She was not prepared, however, for the look of horror in the Marchioness's face as she asked :

"He is not a journalist?"

"No, no. He writes books."

She knew as she spoke that the Marchioness had been

afraid that the story of her secret marriage would somehow appear in the newspapers.

"They are almost as frightened of me as I am of them," Larentia thought, and knew the situation could be funny if she were not so nervous of making a mistake.

"What sort of books?"

Again it was easier to tell the truth.

"My .. uncle is an .. historian."

"So that is why you know so much about mediaeval times!" the Duke said, "and you have certainly come to the right place to learn more."

The Marchioness gave him a look which showed Larentia that she thought he was being far too pleasant and getting away from the point of the conversation.

"His Grace tells me, Miss King," she said, "that you are asking for the enormous sum of £5,000 in return for keeping your marriage a secret. There is of course a very unpleasant word attributed to such a request. It is 'blackmail'!"

It was, Larentia knew, what she had thought herself, but because of the way it was said, she felt it was an insult, and one she resented.

She thought how good Katie had been in keeping her sacred word of honour and it made her reply most angrily:

"I did not blackmail His Grace after he .. left me, and I have no wish to blackmail you, My Lady, or .. anybody else. All I am asking for, is the money which I was .. promised, and I have suggested it would be more convenient if the debt was paid off once and for all, rather than month by month."

"We have first to establish of course, that the 'debt' as you call it, is real, and that your marriage to the Duke actually took place."

"Why should you doubt it?" Larentia asked, "when I have brought you the Marriage Certificate?"

She tried to speak defensively, but even to herself her voice sounded weak and fearful.

"I am sure, Miss King, you understand," the Duke interrupted, "that we not only have to ask questions, but also to reassure ourselves that the late Duke, who is no longer with us, actually married you in such a surprising fashion."

"Why he . . did so was made very . . clear in the . . letter," Larentia said.

"Letters have been forged before now," the Marchioness remarked.

The words startled Larentia and for the first time she wondered if the letter was a forgery.

Then, as she thought about it, she was aware that the paper on which it was written was not very impressive nor, as might have been expected, was it surmounted with an elaborate crest or coat-of-arms.

One thing she had noticed while going round the Castle was that the Tregarons were proud of their heraldic quarterings.

On almost every picture either the arms of the Garon of the time were painted on his shield or he stood beside them.

There were shields on the stone staircase, on the mantelpiece in the Library, on the ceiling of the room in which they were now talking, and on every tomb in the ancient Chapel she had visited with Mr. Webster.

It seemed strange that the Duke should therefore have written to Katie on plain paper and what was more, Larentia thought, the paper itself, while of a good quality, had not been particularly creased or dirty in any way.

Katie must have kept it for six years, and even if she had wrapped it up or locked it away in a writing-box, surely it would not look so fresh and unsullied?

These thoughts raced through her brain, then she told herself that even if the Marchioness had made her slightly suspicious of the letter there was still the Marriage Certificate and Harry Carrington had said the marriage had been inscribed in the Register of Southwark Cathedral.

She lifted her chin and said quietly :

"If Your Ladyship is in any doubt it would be wisest for you to visit Southwark Cathedral and see the evidence in the Marriage Register, as that was where the wedding took place."

"What I am trying to understand," the Marchioness said, "is why you consented to keep the marriage a secret? Surely you must have felt very proud that you, who are of no importance, and on the stage, should become a Duchess?"

"I did it because it was what His Grace asked me to do," Larentia said quietly.

The Duke, listening, thought she had certainly scored a point not by what she had said, but by the way she had said it.

The Marchioness glanced at the Duke as if she was asking him to help her in what she wished to ask next.

"I think, Miss King," the Duke said, after a moment's slightly uncomfortable silence, "that it would be best to wait while we investigate your claim and discuss what arrangements should be made for the future when they are completely substantiated."

He saw the look of horror which came in Larentia's eyes.

"Are you .. suggesting .. Your Grace .. that I am to .. wait perhaps for quite a .. long time while you visit the Cathedral to inspect the Marriage Register and make other enquiries?"

"That and I suppose there must be people who have seen you and the Duke together and were aware of your relationship?"

"You cannot .. make me wait so long!" Larentia cried. "I have already told you I have to return to London to be with .. my uncle. It may take days .. perhaps weeks for you to find out what you want to know .. and by that time he may .. die without me."

"If he is really as ill as that," the Duke remarked, "how were you able to leave him?"

"He is being looked after temporarily," Larentia said quickly, "but I have to go back and..please..if you will not give me all the..money I have asked for..could I have the..money for my..debt?"

"If your claim is substantiated, Miss King, you will certainly be entitled to the £5,000 that you have demanded, or perhaps, it depends upon what the Lawyers decide, a monthly settlement will be made available to you. But until we have more proof than what you have provided with these two documents, then I am afraid there is nothing we can do but wait."

"But I have told you that is..impossible!" Larentia said. "Please..Your Grace..let me have the smaller amount of money. It cannot matter so very much to you ..but it matters more than I can possibly explain..to me."

As she spoke she saw the face of Isaac Levy quite clearly and his greedy eyes!

She knew that if he was defrauded not only of the money he had loaned them, but also of his exorbitant amount of interest, he would take his revenge in a way she did not dare contemplate.

Supposing he should hurt her father when he came out of the Nursing Home? Supposing he seized their house and all their possessions?

Larentia had not lived in a poor neighbourhood without knowing how cruelly the impoverished could be treated when they owed money to their landlords, to a publican, or even to their neighbours.

Men were beaten up or even murdered for what seemed a trifling sum, and from what she had seen of the Usurer she had the feeling he would stick at nothing when it came to losing his money.

"Please..please," she pleaded now, "help me and I.. swear I will not make any trouble for you or..do anything you do not..wish me to do."

The Duke rose abruptly to his feet.

"I think, Aunt Muriel," he said, "there is nothing to be

gained by Miss King upsetting herself any further. Perhaps we are all a little overwrought by the surprise of this news, and later in the day we should again talk quietly and calmly and see what can be done to the advantage of us all."

"I really do not think there is anything to discuss, Justin," the Marchioness replied. "Miss King may be in a hurry to receive her money; that of course is understandable and there may be a good explanation for it. At the same time, we have to safeguard ourselves against fraud and trickery. But as you suggest, we will leave things as they are until later this afternoon. I, for one, feel extremely upset at what has transpired."

The Marchioness rose and without looking again at Larentia she turned and walked with great dignity towards the door.

The Duke opened it for her and only when he had shut it behind her did he look back to see that Larentia, having risen from the chair in which she had been sitting, was standing looking at him with such an expression of tragedy in her eyes, that it was infinitely pathetic.

There was too, he thought, as he walked back towards her something very helpless in her attitude.

It struck him that she was not a hard-boiled, scheming Gaiety Girl as the Marchioness would argue, but instead somebody young and bewildered and quite unequipped to know how to cope with the situation in which she found herself.

Then he told himself he was being ridiculous.

She was an actress and why should he expect she would not be able to act?

Then as he stood beside her, she looked up at him, her eyes met his, and she said in a broken little voice that was hardly above a whisper:

"Help .. please .. help me .. I do not know .. what to do!"

Chapter Five

Larentia was sitting in the sunshine on a grass incline that led up to the Keep.

Because the sun was so hot, she had taken off her bonnet and the shawl which she had put over her shoulders and Tennyson's poem of the Holy Grail was on her lap.

She was reading the words carefully, feeling that somehow they held a message for her, but she was not certain exactly what she would find.

She only knew that the words created pictures in her mind which were somehow linked with the beauty of the Castle and the atmosphere of mysticism which was inescapable wherever she went or looked.

For the moment she had forgotten her own troubles and difficulties and was swept away into an ancient land of the past where Arthur's Knights rode out to save and rescue the women who were menaced by evil in any form, whether that of a Dragon or a sorcerer.

'That is what I need to save me,' Larentia thought and saw the Duke walking towards her over the green grass.

She had known when she appealed to him in the Morning-Room that although it was against his common sense he wanted to help her.

For a moment she thought he was going to reply that he would give her the money she had asked for and let her return to London.

Then he had said:

"May I think about what you have asked me, and let you know later in the day? I do appreciate your sense of urgency and the reason for it, but I also have to do what is right and fair towards my family."

"Yes .. of course you .. must."

She knew what he was saying was wise and, in fact, just, but rather irrationally she was disappointed.

She realised when she ate her luncheon alone in the room where she had breakfasted that the Marchioness was refusing to associate with her.

She told herself it was what she should have expected, instead of believing, as she had, that perhaps an older woman would be sympathetic because Katie King was young and ignorant.

Thinking back into the past Larentia was aware how bitterly her mother's relatives had disapproved of her marrying her father because he was poor and had nothing to recommend him except his academic distinction, which, in their eyes, did not count for much.

Her mother's family lived in the North of England and could trace their ancestry back for hundreds of years.

Although they were certainly not the social equal of the Garons, they were gentlefolk and had their roots in an estate that had been theirs for many centuries.

Larentia could remember her grandfather, a very auto-cratic old gentleman, who barked out orders to his children and to his servants in the same way that he had ordered about the Regiment he commanded.

Her mother's two brothers were at the moment in India, serving their country as their father had done before them but Larentia had not seen either of them for over seven years.

When her grandfather had died most of the estate had been sold and the money went to his sons. His daughter, Larentia's mother, received a very small allowance and the capital was held in trust for Larentia when she came of age.

It brought in a little over a hundred pounds a year, which was all she and her father had to live on when his books no longer sold and his Publishers would make no further advance towards the next one.

Larentia was well aware that there was no use appealing to her father's Lawyers to let her have more than they sent her every quarter, because they would merely reply that she must wait until she came of age before she touched any of the capital.

Before Harry Carrington had made the suggestion that she could earn the money for her father's operation by pretending to be Katie King, she had wondered despairingly what, when he was dead, she would do, and where she could go.

She had a number of cousins living somewhere in the North of England, but her mother had always said they were poor and she was quite certain they would not wish to add to their own families already living with them.

She had told herself she must find employment of some sort, but she had no idea what she could do, having no saleable qualifications except that of being able to run a house fairly competently for her father.

The way the Duke lived was a revelation and the extravagance of the food alone made her keep thinking that the money she had asked for to save her father's life and Katie King's was merely a 'drop in the ocean' compared to his annual expenditure.

At breakfast she had been offered a choice of six different dishes, and there had been a bowl of the hot-house fruit on a side-table besides the silver coffee set which appeared to Larentia to be the epitome of luxury.

At luncheon course succeeded course until it was impossible to eat any more.

Once again as the crested silver dishes were removed by two footmen she thought how little £800 actually meant to the Duke, and how easy it would be for him to give it to her and let her go.

When she had finished her meal she had walked through the corridors looking at the priceless pictures, the fine furniture, the carved console tables and the chests inlaid with ivory and priceless marbles.

The contrast between all this and the life where she must count every halfpenny for fear that she would not be able to get another one, seemed ludicrous.

By the time she walked out into the sunshine she was praying desperately that the Duke would be generous and she could return to London free from the menace of Isaac Levy.

Then when she had opened Tennyson's book of poems she forgot for the moment everything but the music of his words.

"A way by love that waken'd love within,
To answer that which came . . ."

She said the words aloud to herself, saw the Duke walking towards her and waited for the answer that she felt he was bringing her.

She did not move and the sun dazzled her eyes so that she thought as she had seen him before he was "arrayed in silver-shining armour, starry clear".

He reached her side and looking down at her head silhouetted against the dark stone of the Keep, he said:

"I somehow expected to find you here."

"I thought it was an .. appropriate place to .. read the book you .. lent me."

"I brought it to the Castle for the same reason."

Larentia was suddenly aware that she was sitting while the Duke was standing, and as if he read her thoughts when she made a little movement as if she would rise, he lowered himself on to the grass beside her.

She felt he had something to tell her, and she waited, her eyes on his face, thinking how clear-cut his features were and how she had already seen his face a hundred times in the portraits which hung on the walls of the Castle.

"There was a Sir Justin Garon who built this castle," she said impulsively. "Do you sometimes feel as if he is still here?"

She was not certain why she asked the question, it came to her lips without her considering what she should say.

The Duke turned to look at her and after a moment's hesitation he replied:

"Perhaps that is over-simplifying what I actually feel about Sir Justin and my other ancestors who have lived here. I am certainly vividly aware of the atmosphere they have left behind them."

"That is what I feel too," Larentia said. "I am sure they were good because there is nowhere in the Castle that I have been where I have sensed either evil or anything malignant."

The Duke did not look surprised, instead he said quietly:

"Do you always feel an atmosphere as clearly as that?"

"Very often," Larentia replied.

She was thinking as she spoke of what she had felt when she visited Oxford with her father and he had shown her around the ancient Colleges which were redolent with history, and in Cambridge King's College Chapel remained a vivid picture of beauty and sanctity.

Once he had given a lecture to a number of scholars in the British Museum and afterwards she felt as if many of the exhibits spoke to her in a way that only her father would understand.

"I think perhaps you must be of Celtic origin," the Duke said with a smile. "The Celts, especially the Irish, the Scottish and the Welsh are always 'fey', and have developed their senses in a way the English have lamentably failed to do."

"You have just spoken as if you were a Celt yourself."

"My mother was Irish," the Duke replied, "and my grandmother Welsh. I sometimes think their perception is constantly at war with the plain common sense of my English forebears!"

Larentia laughed.

"Who wins the battle?"

"At the moment," the Duke replied, and his eyes were

twinkling, "the Celts are definitely victorious."

They sat talking for perhaps half-an-hour, and Larentia asked the Duke to tell her the legends of his family.

She found he told them well, actually making her see the past come alive so that she felt that they suffered all the ambitions, anxieties and the disappointments of ordinary life as if he was feeling it himself.

Then as she talked with an ease that she had never known before in the company of a stranger, she saw a servant walking towards them across the lawn.

The Duke saw him too and gave a little sigh.

"I am expecting one of my neighbours to visit me this afternoon," he said, "and I must go back, but I hope that tonight you will dine with me."

Larentia looked at him in surprise and he explained:

"I am afraid my aunt does not feel very friendly towards you. She has therefore informed me that as both the news of her brother's death and his secret marriage has upset her, she wishes to retire to her room and will not join me again."

The Duke waited and after a moment Larentia said in a low voice:

"I would .. like to .. dine with Your Grace .. if you are .. sure it is the .. right thing for me to .. do."

"It is what I wish you to do," the Duke answered, "and we could not only continue our conversation which I have greatly enjoyed, but also discuss, as I know you would wish to, your future."

"Then I should very much like to dine with Your Grace," Larentia replied.

The Duke smiled down at her, then he walked away to join the footman.

He was obviously informed that the visitor had arrived, and he strode towards the entrance door into the Castle.

Once again Larentia thought he might be a Knight obeying an urgent summons to ride off and right a wrong.

That evening as she was putting on the only evening-gown she possessed, she thought it would be exciting, if she were not pretending to be somebody else, but could be herself, to be dining alone with a man.

It was something she had never done and she wondered what her father would think if he knew what she was doing, or indeed where she was.

Even though she could talk of other things she knew that some part of her was all the time praying that his operation would be successful so that when she returned to London she would find he was on the road to recovery and they could be together again.

He had, of course, been curious as to who his benefactor might be.

"I can only think, Papa," Larentia had said, "that Dr. Medwin must have talked to somebody who talked to somebody else, and one of the people who admire you for your work in Mediaeval History has decided to do the generous thing."

"It is extremely kind," the Professor had said, "so kind that when I am home again I must make every effort to discover who this 'Good Samaritan' is, and of course, although it will be difficult, to repay him."

Larentia did not reply that that would be impossible, and she took great care not to let her father know exactly what the fee had been.

When he had asked she merely told him vaguely that Dr. Medwin had arranged it with Mr. Sheldon Curtis and all they need concern themselves with was that he was to be operated on by Joseph Lister's pupil, the most skilful Surgeon in the whole of London.

"As you know, I have always admired Lister tremendously," the Professor said with satisfaction, "and I am certain that in the future he will be acclaimed as the great man he undoubtedly is."

"And you will be one of the people who will be able to testify to his success in preventing sepsis," Larentia said and knew that her father was delighted at the idea.

When she was dressed and looked at herself in the mirror,

she did not see for the moment her own reflection, but instead her father's face pale with pain, trying not to let her know the agony he was experiencing.

'I should be with him,' she thought.

She told herself that somehow by the end of the evening she had to persuade the Duke to give her the money and let her go back to London.

Because she was thinking only of her father, she had no idea how becoming the very simple white gown she had made herself was, when she was wearing it.

It was a very cheap material which fitted her closely, and billowed out behind in a very small, but nevertheless fashionable bustle which she had copied from one of the sketches in a magazine.

She thought it was extravagant of her to spend even the few shillings the material had cost when they were so hard up.

But she had nothing to wear in the evening for her father, who always changed for dinner, and she knew it distressed him to see her in shabby and threadbare garments and to feel it was his fault that she could not afford to be better dressed.

She had, therefore, stitched away diligently until the gown was finished and because it was made on almost classical lines, a tight bodice outlining her small breasts and tiny waist, the skirt drawn back to reveal the curve of her hips, she looked to the Duke even more than ever the embodiment of Diana, as she walked into the Salon where he was waiting.

Then as she looked at him she gave an almost inaudible gasp.

She had seen her father in evening-clothes, and the audiences to which she had occasionally read his lectures when he was unable to read them himself had for the most part been wearing evening-dress.

But scholars were one thing and the Duke was certainly another.

While he was impressive enough in the daytime, in the

evening he had a grandeur that made Larentia feel that he came from another sphere.

She walked slowly towards him, then when he smiled she made a respectful curtsy which gave her a grace that he expected.

"What have you been doing all the afternoon?" he asked.

It was almost as if he forced himself to speak to her in an ordinary manner, but his eyes resting on her hair said something very different.

"I have been .. reading and .. thinking, Your Grace."

"That is what I would have liked to be doing with you," he replied, "but unfortunately I had to listen to a long, rather aggressive dissertation on local politics."

"I expect somebody was asking you to put forward the Farmers' claims in the House of Lords," Larentia said perceptively.

"That is correct," the Duke admitted, "but I did not expect you, living in London, to know about country problems."

With difficulty Larentia prevented herself from telling him that when her mother was alive, they had not lived in London, but in Hertfordshire where they had a small house in a quiet village which had been a perfect place for her father to write his books without being disturbed.

It was only when her mother had died that her father had come to London, because when he was lecturing and researching in the Libraries and Museums he had not liked to leave her alone.

"I still prefer the country," Larentia said, after a little pause.

"And yet you have chosen a life that is exactly the opposite of such an inclination," the Duke said accusingly. "In the country, as you know, we go out in the daytime and go to bed early, and you do the very opposite."

It was almost as if he was accusing her of being unfaithful to her own heart and after a moment Larentia said:

"There are reasons why I do not want to explain what I do, so let us talk about you, Your Grace, and your Castle."

"We spoke of that this afternoon. I think it is my turn now to ask you about yourself."

"No .. please," Larentia pleaded.

To her relief at that moment dinner was announced.

They dined in the big Dining-Room as the Duke had not yet arranged for the meals to be served in the smaller room he preferred which had been shut up for some years.

Larentia was fascinated by the huge room, the beauty of its arched ceiling and the carved Musicians' Gallery at one end of it.

She felt as if she was acting a part in a play, and what frightened her was that she might make a mistake in her lines and make the Duke suspicious that she was not what she pretended to be.

Because she knew he was interested she told him stories of King Arthur that he did not know, and they argued as she might have argued with her father, as to the validity of the French sources.

These, for some reason she had never understood, had included since the 12th century, many Arthurian tales in circulation.

Only when the servants had left the room and the Duke was sitting back in his carved chair, a glass of brandy in his hand, did he say:

"I am bewildered, Miss King."

"Why?" Larentia enquired.

"That seeing your unusual, extraordinary knowledge of Mediaeval History and your familiarity with both French and Welsh, you choose to earn your living on the stage."

Because she had forgotten for the moment that she was not herself, Larentia looked at him and tried to find a plausible answer.

It took her some seconds before she managed to say:

"I do not think that .. anything we have .. talked about tonight .. is particularly saleable."

"On the contrary," the Duke argued, "I am sure there are many historians who would welcome with open arms, an assistant, or a secretary, who knows as much as you do about their work."

Larentia longed to inform him that he was wrong.

Most historians like her father were too impoverished to afford a secretary and any work she did for such men would have to be given free.

She did not speak and after a moment the Duke said:

"I suppose it is because you are so beautiful that you feel you need the plaudits of the crowd, rather than the appreciation of one writer."

He saw the surprise in Larentia's eyes at the compliment. Then she looked away to say:

"It is not .. easy for a woman to .. earn money in what is very much a .. man's world."

"That is as it should be," the Duke said, "for a man surely should keep a woman and, if it were possible, no woman should have to work."

"Even when this Castle was built," Larentia said, trying to speak lightly, "there were women who worked in it whether they were scrubbing and cleaning, sewing or looking after children."

"Yes, of course," the Duke agreed, "but they did not look like you!"

The way he spoke brought the colour to her cheeks and to his surprise he saw that she was shy.

He bent forward first to put his glass down on the table, before he said:

"Many men must have told you how lovely you are, but I feel this is exactly the right setting for your beauty because here I can imagine you have just stepped into Camelot."

What he said made Larentia feel even more embarrassed than she had before, and because she felt that somehow she ought not to sit listening to him she replied quickly:

"I think..perhaps..Your Grace..I am at fault..in not leaving you..now that..dinner is finished."

"There is no point in your leaving me," the Duke said, "and I do not wish you to do so, but I think we might return to the Salon."

Larentia rose quickly to her feet and he opened the door for her and they walked in silence down the wide corridor.

Then they reached the Salon where candles were lit making the huge room seem even lovelier than it did in the day-time.

There was a fire burning in the grate and Larentia moved towards it to hold out her hands towards the flames.

"You are cold?" the Duke asked.

"My fingers..are cold."

She knew that really she was nervous, and yet it was not a frightening nervousness, but an exciting one and something she had never encountered before.

It made her feel tinglingly alive because he was beside her, and she was acutely conscious of him as a man.

"I am behaving stupidly!" she told herself, "because previously I have never been in such a position."

But she knew it was far more than that; something that it was hard to put into words; and yet it was indisputably an emotion that vibrated through her, that seemed to come from him and link her to him.

The Duke stood close beside her. She was aware that he was looking at her hair, and because she felt as if he was speaking to her without words, she said:

"I..I feel you are..criticising me."

"I am admiring you!" the Duke said firmly. "Do you object?"

"I.it makes me..shy."

"How can you be shy? You intrigue me, Larentia, and I am beginning to think that you have cast a spell over me from which it is difficult for me to escape."

"If Merlin were here he would..tell you how to..do so."

"But he is not here," the Duke replied. "Therefore I am in your thrall."

Larentia tried to laugh, but her eyes could not meet the Duke's.

Then as she wanted to move away from him she was unable to do so.

"Look at me, Larentia!" the Duke said unexpectedly.

Because there was a note of command in his voice she obeyed him and as their eyes met he said very softly:

"Why are you so mysterious? Tell me the truth about yourself!"

Larentia knew she should say that she had told him the truth, and yet somehow the lie would not come to her lips.

Instead some words she had been reading this afternoon came insistently to her mind, almost as though the Duke spoke them aloud.

> *"While thus he spake, his eye dwelling on mine*
> *Drew me, with power upon me, till I grew*
> *One with him to believe as he believed."*

"One with him!"

She could not take her eyes from the Duke's and she knew that his power drew her and she was in fact his prisoner whether she wished it or not.

Very slowly, almost as if it was a movement that was part music rather than a human volition, the Duke put his arms around Larentia and drew her against him.

Their eyes still looked into each other's and she was hardly aware what he was doing or whether he or she had moved.

She only knew that she was one with him and it was something she had been in the past, would be in the future, and nothing could prevent their coming together.

He drew her closer still, then his lips were on hers and he felt the little quiver that went through her and knew it vibrated within himself.

To Larentia it was more powerful, a dream that she had felt enveloping her since they had talked together outside the Keep and she had found it impossible to be free of him, even when he was not there.

Now as his lips touched hers she was kissed for the first time in her life and thought it was as she had expected it to be.

The surrendering of herself to a man who dominated her because he was a man, and who took not only her body, but also her soul into his keeping, and she could not prevent him from doing so.

She knew it was not only the Duke who held her captive. It was also the mystery of the Castle and the Knights who had lived in it, and the legendary magic which had remained within it all down the centuries.

It was all there in the strange rapture he aroused in her that she felt pulsating through her and knew it was what she had felt when she had read of King Arthur himself, his deeds of valour and heroism.

The Duke drew her into a mystical world that she had always sensed, yet had never been fully a part of, until now.

Because it was so perfect and was, to her, the finding of the Holy Grail which she had sought and longed for, she felt that he carried her up to God and they were no longer human, but divine.

The Duke's lips became more insistent, more demanding, and yet there was a kind of reverence that she had always known must be the real love if ever she found it.

It was the love she had imagined and which had been expressed in the Arthurian legends, and yet now was real, as real as she was herself, and as real as he was.

At the same time he was all her secret dreams rolled into one.

He held her closer still and she felt as if a sudden shaft of sunshine swept through her, burning its way from her lips to her breasts.

Then he raised his head and she almost cried aloud because she was losing the ecstasy he had given her.

"You have bewitched me," the Duke said, and his voice was unsteady.

She made a little murmur and hid her face against his shoulder.

"How could you come to me looking like Diana, whose portrait I have loved since I first saw it, and never believed that any woman could look the same?"

He felt Larentia quiver against him and he kissed her hair before he said :

"You are so lovely! So exquisitely lovely, and I know that I must look after you, and whatever you have done in the past, your future is with me."

He put his fingers under her chin and turned her face up to his.

What do you feel about me?" he asked. "Tell me, although I think I already know the answer."

As if he compelled her to say it, Larentia murmured :

"I .. love you .. and I .. cannot help it! I have loved you .. ever since I .. first saw you in .. 'silver-shining armour starry clear' !"

The Duke smiled.

"You really thought I looked like that?"

"That was .. how you .. *did* look!"

"And to me you were Diana as I worshipped her in the picture by Boucher every time I went to Paris. How could you have hair like hers?"

He put up his hand to touch it as he spoke. Then as if he was afraid of finding that she was not after all human, he was kissing her again.

He kissed her wildly, insistently, passionately, until she felt as if the fire in him awoke a flickering fire within herself and little flames mounted within her breast towards her lips...

A long time passed before the Duke drew Larentia to a sofa and they sat down side by side.

"I find it hard to think of anything but you, my darling one," he said, "but it is something we have to do and I believe it would be best if I took you back to London tomorrow."

For a moment she found it hard to understand what he was saying, then as the meaning of his words percolated through her mind she gave a little cry.

"You know I have to go to London as .. quickly as .. possible."

"I will take you," he said, "and when we reach there we will find a place where we can be together."

He saw the question in her eyes and said with a smile:

"You said you loved me, and I love you! Nothing else for the moment is of consequence, but I shall not allow you to go back on the stage, and ..."

He stopped, then almost as if he had forgotten it until this moment he said:

"Now will you tell me the truth, and if you were really married to my uncle? It is something I cannot believe for the simple reason that I would swear if I could on the Sword of Excalibur that you have never been kissed by anyone but me."

Larentia drew in her breath.

She was trying to come back to earth from the clouds of glory where the Duke had carried her.

Suddenly afraid she tried to remember that she was not herself, not Larentia, and not with a man who had been sent to her by God.

She was Katie King, the Gaiety Girl who had married secretly another Duke who was now dead.

"Tell me," the Duke insisted.

She knew he was tempting her, asking her to break her word to Harry Carrington, and most of all to the task she had set herself of earning the money which would save two people's lives.

With a superhuman effort that was agonising, she moved from the shelter of the Duke's arms.

"You said you would .. take me to London," she said. "Please .. I cannot answer questions until .. then."

She rose as she spoke and walked towards the fire and the Duke, still sitting on the sofa, watched her.

"You are admitting you have a secret, Larentia," he said. "Do you want me to make a bargain with you? I will give you the money you want if I can take you to London, and you will then tell me everything I want to know."

"I am .. not certain what it is you .. do want to .. know," Larentia said evasively, "but I promise that I will answer your .. questions once I am in London and I have .. the £800 to pay my .. debt."

She thought as she spoke that she defamed the very love that he had given her and which had made her, for one moment, touch the wings of ecstasy.

Never had she known she was capable of feeling such sensations, of having her very soul lifted out of her body.

But while her heart told her one thing, her mind told her that she must do what she had come to do, and that she could not cheat on either her father or Katie King whose lives had been saved by the money loaned them by Isaac Levy.

Whatever her own dreams, whatever her love for the Duke that seemed to fill the whole universe, she must behave in an honourable manner and not by telling him the truth betray those who trusted her.

And yet she felt because she had loved him and because he was just sitting looking at her, that she might have lost him and she turned round.

"Please understand," she begged, "I love you .. I love you .. more than I can .. ever put into words .. but .. I cannot tell you what you want to know .. now."

"It is of no consequence," the Duke replied. "The only thing that matters is that you have said you love me, and unless you are the best actress the world has ever known, I believe you."

"It is .. true," Larentia answered.

He rose then, and walked towards her to hold her closely against him.

"Tell me," he said, "make me believe it. Say it so that I can understand it!"

"I love you .. I love you! I did not .. know that love was .. like this."

"Like what?"

"That it is .. holy and given to us by .. God!"

The Duke looked down into her eyes, then once again his lips were on hers and just for one moment Larentia was frightened that the magic had gone.

But again it was there, pulsating through her, vibrating in the air around them, joining them closely until they were one and nothing could divide them.

The Duke kissed her until she was compliant in his arms, then he kissed her closed eyes, the softness of her cheeks, then her lips again.

"I cannot wait for you," he said, and his voice was deep with desire. "As soon as we arrive in London I will buy a house where we can be together and you shall have everything you want, my precious. Every comfort that it is possible for me to give you."

It was difficult for Larentia to understand what he was saying.

But she heard him talk of a house and thought she must tell him that she had to look after her father when he left the Nursing Home, and that she would not spend a great deal of time with the Duke, however much she wished to do so.

She wanted to explain, but told herself it was impossible at the moment while he thought it was her uncle who was ill, and not her father.

How could she tell him she was not Katie King, but Larentia Braintree, and it was not a question of her giving up the stage on which she had never appeared.

It was all too much to think about, too much to consider when his voice was sending little thrills through her, and she was vividly conscious of how closely he was holding her and that her lips were aching for his.

She wanted as she had never wanted anything in her life for him to possess her mouth, but the Duke slowly and reluctantly set her free.

"You must go to bed now, my darling," he said. "If we are to catch the early train to London it means we must leave here very early, at eight o'clock and I must make the arrangements."

"Y . yes .. of course."

"Because I do not wish you to be worried," he went on, "I promise that when we start our journey I will give you the cheque which you have asked for and later when we reach London we can discuss all the other problems."

Larentia did not trust her voice to reply.

The Duke rose and drew her to her feet.

"Go to bed and dream of me," he said. "Do not worry. Leave everything in my hands, I promise that I will look after you and I swear that whatever the difficulties I will not give you up or lose you."

"You .. really .. want me?"

"I will answer that question a thousand times over in the future," the Duke replied.

His voice was suddenly serious as he added :

"It is not going to be easy, my darling, but just as you have kept your marriage a secret for so long, I think we can manage to keep our love a secret from those who would be horrified and shocked if it was known we were together."

His voice deepened and strengthened as if he convinced himself as he said :

"No-one will know, and although you may miss the stage a little at first, I swear to you our happiness will make up for everything."

Larentia was still not aware of what he was suggesting.

It was so difficult to think of anything but how handsome he was and she still felt as if she was floating on air and he was not the Duke of Tregaron but one of Arthur's Knights, or even King Arthur himself.

Nothing was real except her love for him, nothing was understandable except that she had found what she had always been seeking, and she was no longer alone or frightened.

She was one with him and his power drew her and held her.

The Duke put his arm around her shoulders and they moved slowly across the Salon side by side.

As they reached the door he kissed first her forehead, then her hair.

"Do not worry about anything," he said. "Leave everything in my hands. You belong to me! You are mine, and I will find a solution for everything."

He looked down into her eyes and added:

"Just remember that I love you and you love me!"

She thought he would kiss her again, but instead with what she knew, because she was so closely attuned to him, was a considerable effort, he opened the door.

Obedient to what he required of her, she walked through it and only as she moved away towards the Great Hall did she realise that he was not following her but had remained alone in the Salon.

Chapter Six

Seated opposite the Duke in the train Larentia was travelling in a very different manner from the way in which she had arrived.

They had left the Castle at eight o'clock in a comfortable carriage drawn by four horses, and when they reached the Railway Station the Station Master was waiting for them, resplendent in gold braid and a top-hat, to escort them to a reserved carriage.

There was also one for the servants who accompanied them to see to the luggage and to place a large picnic basket on another seat in their compartment together with a number of newspapers and magazines.

There was a rug to cover Larentia's legs and a servant stood outside the carriage until the last minute before the train left in case the Duke wished to give an order.

Only when they were on their way did he smile at Larentia in a manner which made her heart turn over and say:

"I feel as if we are starting off on an adventure into the unknown, just you and me, and the idea excites me."

Larentia wanted to say it excited her too, but she could not add that she had lain awake most of the night, first in a rapture of love and happiness but then beset by anxiety and the unassailable conviction that when they reached London she must never see the Duke again.

Only when she was alone in the darkness did she go over what he had said to her and understand after a lot of thought exactly what he had meant when he said:

"I will buy a house where we can be together."

Larentia, despite her extensive reading, was very ignorant about love, but she was aware that women had lovers and some of the things she had heard when her father's contemporaries forgot that she was listening, had made her realise why actresses were considered fast and improper.

Men to whom they had not been introduced took them out to supper, gave them jewellery and quite certainly made love to them.

What this actually entailed Larentia did not understand, but she knew that it was wrong and a sin unless they were married to the man concerned, and if they were not, they became 'fallen women', whom the Prime Minister tried to reform.

It was all rather complicated and confused in her mind, except that when she thought it over, she realised that if she agreed to what the Duke had suggested she would become a 'fallen woman'.

At first she could hardly believe that was what he had meant. Then as she went over and over the words he had spoken she remembered all too vividly what he had said:

"I think we can manage to keep our love a secret from those who would be horrified and shocked if it were known that we were together."

Horrified, because they believed her to be the widow of his uncle, and shocked because their love was wrong and wicked when they could not be married.

It was impossible for Larentia at first to acknowledge that the love she had for the Duke, the love which had carried her into a miraculous Heaven, could be anything but pure and good.

Then she remembered that the love the Knight Lancelot had for Queen Guinevere, the wife of King Arthur, had been a guilty one and she had lived only to expiate her wickedness and live down the sin in her heart.

"How could what I feel for the Duke be wrong?" Larentia asked.

Then almost as if God Himself gave her the answer, she

knew that the love which came from the depths of her heart and soul, was not wrong.

What would be wrong was to agree to what the Duke suggested, to allow him to make her his, as he wished to do, so that they became one with their bodies as well as being, as they were now, one with their minds.

"I shall have to disappear," Larentia decided at length.

Then she cried out at the agony of knowing that she must tear herself apart from the man to whom she belonged, whose heart beat as her heart, and who had taken her very soul from between her lips and made it his.

"I love him! I love him!" she cried despairingly into her pillow.

But she knew that she could not lure him into sin, and to do so would spoil the silver-shining armour in which she had first seen him and which she knew was the vibration of his noble spirit.

"Pure love must not be defiled."

She did not know where she had read the words, but now they seemed to be spoken aloud.

Then at the thought of losing the Duke she wept until she fell asleep.

In her dreams she saw his handsome face as he looked at her with an expression she had never seen in a man's eyes before, and she told herself she could never leave him.

She thought if she could explain to him later that she was not Katie King, not a married woman and not an actress, then everything would be different.

Then she knew things would not be better, but worse.

How could the Duke be expected to forgive her not only for frightening him and his family with the information that his uncle the Duke was married, but also for obtaining from him, under false pretences, the sum of £800 that she needed so desperately for her father's operation and Katie's?

They had both breakfasted in their own rooms and when

she had come down the stairs dressed in her dark travelling-cloak with a small bonnet on her shining hair, the Duke had taken her hand-bag from her and put into it an envelope which he held in his hand.

She knew what it contained, but when she would have thanked him, he merely drew her across the Hall and helped her down the steps and into the carriage.

Once again she tried to say thank you, but he put his hand over hers and said:

"I want you to forget everything today except that we are together."

Because his touch made her quiver she could only look at him and feel that it was unnecessary to express her love in words because he knew what she was feeling, just as she was aware that he felt the same.

Now as he looked at her sitting opposite him on the train the Duke thought it impossible to believe that any woman could look so lovely in such mundane surroundings or for him exactly as she was portrayed in the picture of Diana.

He adored her small straight nose, her winged eyebrows, her soft oval face, and, of course, her shining redgold hair.

He longed with a passionate desire to see it falling over her shoulders in a cloud of glory.

He knew it must be very long because Larentia had arranged it in thick plaits, looped up at the back of her head and secured on the top by large pins.

He told himself that soon he would undo the plaits and bury his face in the soft silkiness of her golden hair, then draw it over her face like a veil and kiss her lips through it.

Almost as if she could read his thoughts he saw the colour rise in her cheeks.

He asked how it was possible that she could look so shy and untouched, and yet have been married to a man who was as debauched and vicious as his uncle had been.

He tried to thrust the thought from him because it

tortured him to think of Larentia giving even her hand to another man, let alone herself.

Yet he had said to her whatever she had done in the past, must be forgotten, because the present and the future were his, so he would forget – yes, of course he would forget – that he was not, as he would have wished to be, the first man in her life.

His love, he swore to himself, was great enough to prevent the truth from spoiling their happiness!

Because he thought it would be difficult to explain to his aunt why he had left in such haste, the Duke had written the Marchioness a letter.

He told her he had found it expedient to leave for London to investigate Miss King's claim and he would beg her not to mention to anyone what had occurred while she had been at the Castle.

He added:

"As soon as I know more than I do at the moment, I will get in touch with you at your home. Until then, Aunt Muriel, I trust you, as I know you trust me."

He left the note to be taken up to the Marchioness with her breakfast, knowing that although she would be surprised at his departure, she would not have expected to see him so early in the morning.

He felt in fact a feeling of freedom as they set off, and now as the train speeded on its way he told himself he was happier than he had ever been in his whole life.

He did not know why, but all the women he had known, and there had been quite a number of them, had always eventually disappointed him.

Although when he had first kissed them he had thought that the feeling they evoked in him would be different, he had known even while they aroused in him a very human desire that something else was lacking.

But when he had kissed Larentia last night it was quite different from any kiss he had ever given or received before, and the rapture and the divine ecstasy that she felt communicated itself to him so that he felt the same.

Never with any other woman had he felt as if he touched not only the wings of ecstasy, but became part of the divine, and yet that was what Larentia had given him, and as he looked at her now, he wanted to kneel at her feet.

Because the train was noisy it was difficult to talk, but they both felt because they were together that there was little need for words.

The Duke's eyes were continually on Larentia's face. And when she looked at him she knew that they were as close as if she was in his arms.

At noon because they had breakfasted early they opened the picnic basket.

It was filled with so many delicious things that Larentia protested that it was hard to make a choice. But she knew that because the Duke was there anything she ate would taste like ambrosia and when he made her drink a little wine, it was nectar.

She thought that if he imagined she was the Goddess Diana, to her he was god-like himself in his appearance and in the nobility of his mind.

At the first station they stopped after luncheon, one of the servants came to clear away the picnic basket and bring them coffee which had been kept hot in a hay-basket.

"This has been a very luxurious picnic," Larentia teased, remembering how she had been too nervous to go to a station Refreshment-Room on her journey to the Castle.

"It is only the second of many meals we will share," the Duke said, "and, my darling, if I cannot find exactly the right background for you at first you must forgive me. As soon as I reach Garon House I will make arrangements to find something at least adequate so that we need not wait."

When he had finished speaking he was surprised at the blush which swept over Larentia's cheeks and the way in which she turned her head away to look out of the window.

"What is wrong?" he asked.

"Nothing."

He told himself she was shy at the idea of being alone with him, and while he thought she looked more adorable and attractive in her shyness than anything he could imagine, he was puzzled as to why what he had said should have affected her so deeply.

"I have so much to discover about you," he said in his deep voice, "and so much to teach you, my darling, about love."

Insidiously, and he could not prevent it, he had a vision of his uncle's debauched face and the memory of what he had been told of his revolting vices.

For the moment the Duke asked himself if he was insane or whether he was being deceived by an exceptionally brilliant actress.

"Look at me, Larentia!" he ordered sharply.

She turned her face and when her eyes met his he saw in them an expression that was almost one of adoration.

Then because something fastidious in him made him feel that it would somehow belittle their love if he kissed her in the train he merely raised her hands to his lips, kissing first one then the other.

He went back to his seat opposite her, content to know that every time she looked at him her eyes softened and her lips parted as if she found it difficult to breathe.

The train was a fast one stopping at only two stations, and yet when they reached St. Pancras Larentia felt exhausted, not by the journey, but by the knowledge that after today she would never see the Duke again.

She had made up her mind what she must do and planned it very carefully, not only during the night but while he was sitting opposite her, and how she wanted to throw herself into his arms and ask him to kiss her just once more.

"How can I go through life without him?" she asked

herself. "How can I leave him knowing that he is somewhere in the world and I may not see him?"

And yet she knew what she was doing was right, firstly because what he wanted her to do was wicked, and secondly because to confess to him that she had lied and made his acquaintance under false pretences would be to invite his contempt.

She was sure that he was so upright and noble that he would despise all liars, especially women who perjured themselves to extract money from him.

She was vividly conscious of the envelope in her handbag and when she searched for a handkerchief and saw it against her worn purse she wanted to tear it up and tell him she had no right to it.

Then she remembered it belonged not to her but to Isaac Levy, who would be waiting for it with a greedy glint in his eyes because it would bring him a hundred per cent interest on his loan.

"Goodbye, my love, goodbye!" Larentia was saying in her heart, and it was as if the rumble of the wheels beneath her repeated the words over and over again.

Then because she loved the Duke so desperately she opened her lips to tell him the truth – she was not Katie King and having paid her debts she would do what he asked.

If she became his mistress and he made love to her, perhaps it would be even more wonderful than his kisses had been!

Then she was appalled that she could even think such things! What would her father, with his high ideals, think of her?

He had looked after her and protected her, and the knowledge of her belonging to a man to whom she was not married would, she knew, be a greater pain than anything he had suffered from the cancerous growth within his body.

"There is nothing I can do but disappear," Larentia told

herself, and knew that her thoughts had gone round in a full circle and come back to where they had started.

"There will be a carriage waiting for us," the Duke was saying, "because I sent a servant to London on the midnight train telling my Comptroller we were arriving and to have everything in readiness.'

Larentia murmured something and he continued:

"I will drop you off first. I want to see where you live."

Larentia had anticipated that he might wish to take her home and she knew it was something she must prevent.

"I wish to go where my uncle is staying with the friends who have looked after him while I have been away," she replied.

"Yes, of course," the Duke agreed, "and where is that?"

"It is a house in Harley Street."

"That will be easy," he smiled. "Harley Street is on the way from St. Pancras to Berkeley Square."

As the Duke had expected there was one of his senior servants waiting on the platform to escort him and Larentia to a carriage, and they only had to wait for her small trunk.

The rest of the luggage was looked after by the servants who had travelled in the other carriage.

"What is the number in Harley Street?" the Duke asked, as the footman placed a fur-lined rug over Larentia's knees.

"Twenty-nine," she replied.

The door was shut and the carriage started off. The Duke took Larentia's hand in both of his and held it closely.

"May I call for you later this evening," he asked, "and take you out to dinner?"

"I think that .. might be .. difficult."

"Then luncheon tomorrow?"

"That would be wonderful."

"I will call for you at a quarter-to-one."

He gave a little sigh.

"It will be a very long time to wait, but I do understand you have to see your uncle and it may be difficult for you to explain to your friends who I am. Perhaps it would be best if they were not told the truth."

"Y . yes . . of course," Larentia said in a very small voice.

"Oh, my precious, I hate these lies!" the Duke exclaimed. "But I know you understand that it would be a mistake for us to cause a lot of gossip and I am afraid that a Duke is always vulnerable not only to what people say, but also to the newspapers."

"I would certainly not wish to subject you to that," Larentia said quickly.

"Tomorrow we will decide how we can be together at every possible moment," the Duke said.

He gave a little laugh before he went on :

"It seems impossible that I should have fallen so madly, crazily in love when I have known you for such a short time, but actually I have loved you for years. You have always been in my heart."

"I feel too as if I have . . loved you since the . . beginning of . . time," Larentia said.

"That is the real truth," the Duke agreed. "We have been together in other lives, perhaps in other worlds, and now we are only taking up the threads from where we left off when we last parted."

"And that will . . happen again?"

"Let us not talk of being parted in this life," the Duke said. "We shall have many, many years together. Oh, my precious, what is it about you that makes me know you belong to me, and I to you, and nothing can separate us?"

Instinctively Larentia's fingers tightened on his because she knew there were only a few minutes left before they would be separated for ever.

He thought it was not a touch of agony but one of pleasure, and he raised her hand to his lips, kissing first her glove, then pulling it aside to kiss the blue veins of her wrist.

Feeling his lips, the pressure of them, and the closeness of him made her feel as if her heart leapt from her body and her love enveloped him to the point where it was difficult to think of anything but the glory of it.

Then the carriage came to a standstill and they both of them realised with a start that they had reached Harley Street.

"It is .. best that you should .. not be seen," Larentia said hastily, her words a little incoherent, for it was difficult to speak.

"I understand," the Duke said. "Goodbye, my precious one! Take care of yourself until I see you tomorrow."

She tried to smile at him and he saw that her eyes seemed to fill her whole face and were for the moment tragic.

He thought how wonderful it was that she should feel so deeply affected at such a short parting.

"G . good .. bye . . ."

Larentia could hardly breathe the words. Then she stepped out of the carriage and the footman carried her trunk up the steps and into the hall.

A servant was looking at Larentia in astonishment as the trunk was put down. Then the Duke's footman went down the steps again and back to the carriage.

When he was out of ear-shot Larentia said:

"This is 39, Harley Street, is it not?"

"No, Madam, this is twenty-nine, the house of Mr. Frederick Baldwin."

"Oh, how stupid of me!" Larentia exclaimed. "I have come to the wrong address."

The servant had half shut the door, but she could see the carriage had driven away and now she said:

"Number thirty-nine cannot be far. As my carriage has gone I will walk there, and perhaps you will be very kind to keep my trunk until I send somebody to collect it?"

"That will be quite all right, Madam, and number thirty-nine is only five houses up, the street having the odd numbers on this side, and the even ones on the other."

"Thank you," Larentia said. "It was very foolish of me to have made the mistake."

"People often get muddled in this street," the servant remarked confidentially. "What with so many doctors moving in there's callers every minute of the day and night!"

"I can understand how it could cause confusion," Larentia said sympathetically.

The servant opened the door for her and she walked into the street seeing that by this time the Duke's carriage was out of sight.

She passed number thirty-nine and went on to forty-nine where she had been before and asked for Mr. Sheldon Curtis.

Now all the anxiety and worry over her father seemed to sweep over her again and she was suddenly apprehensive that she would learn that his operation had not been successful or perhaps the growth had been too severe for them even to attempt to save his life.

She was shown into a dark impersonal waiting-room, and when she was alone she found herself praying that because she had been happy with the Duke she would not be punished by learning now that she had lost her father.

She knew it was childish to think that life should balance itself out in such a way, but nevertheless the idea persisted because she knew she had been doing something which intrinsically was wrong.

Her love for the Duke had overwhelmed her to the point where for moments of time at any rate, when she was with him, she even forgot how much her father meant to her.

"Oh, please, God .. please let Papa live!" she prayed.

As the door opened and Mr. Curtis came in she could only look at him in a kind of terror in case what she feared had happened.

"I am glad to see you, Miss Braintree," the Surgeon said holding out his hand. "I am sure you have been very anxious about your father while he has been in my care, so

129

I am going to allow you to see him for just two or three minutes."

"T . to .. see him?"

"He has been asking for you when he has been conscious. He is still very drowsy, so I cannot allow you to stay with him for long."

"He is .. all right? The operation was .. successful?"

"I hoped you would trust me," Mr. Curtis said with a smile. "Very successful, Miss Braintree! In fact, everything went exactly as I hoped and your father will soon be back at work and I am looking forward to reading his next book!"

Larentia found it impossible to speak.

Then her relief made her look so lovely that Mr. Curtis thought as they walked up the stairs that she was, without exception, the most beautiful young woman he had ever seen.

The blinds were drawn to keep out the sunshine, but Larentia could see her father looking pale but extremely handsome as he lay on his bed.

She went to his bedside and took his hand in hers.

"Papa!" she said softly.

He did not move, and after a moment Mr. Curtis said: "Speak to him again."

"Papa! I am here!" Larentia said in a louder tone.

Now there was a smile on the Professor's lips and his eyes opened slowly.

"Larentia! Are you – all right?"

"Quite all right, Papa, and so glad, so very, very glad that you are!"

"I will be home – soon – I must – get that book – finished."

"Yes, Papa. We will finish it together."

The Professor shut his eyes and Larentia bent forward to kiss his cheek.

Then as she knew that Mr. Curtis wished her to leave, she followed him silently towards the door.

Outside he said:

"I want to keep your father as quiet as possible during the next few days. Then we will discuss how soon he can come home to you."

"Thank you.. thank you more than I can.. possibly say," Larentia said. "Had it not been for you.. he would have.. died."

"I am afraid that is the truth," Mr. Curtis agreed, "and I intend to send a report about this operation to Mr. Joseph Lister in Edinburgh. I know he will be interested."

He smiled before he added:

"After all, your father is a very famous man, Miss Braintree, and I hope that more and more people will begin to realise that with Lister's methods lives can be saved instead of lost, and we need to keep men like your father alive."

"Thank you," Larentia said again.

"Now do not worry about him," Mr. Curtis went on as they walked down the stairs. "You can come in again tomorrow morning, if you like, and stay with him for about five minutes."

"I will do that," Larentia said. "Can it be early?"

"As early as you like."

"Then I will come, if I may, at about ten o'clock."

"That would suit us all. Goodbye, Miss Braintree. Take care of yourself."

Larentia smiled at him, then as a servant opened the door she said:

"I forgot to ask. Another of Dr. Medwin's patients came in at the same time as my father, a Miss Katie King. How is she?"

There was silence. Then Mr. Curtis said:

"I am sorry to tell you that despite everything I could do, she died this morning!"

He saw the shocked expression on Larentia's face and added:

"The growth in her body had got too much of a hold and

was different from your father's. I do not think even Mr. Lister himself could have saved her."

"I am sure no-one could have done more than you, Mr. Curtis," Larentia said, then added:

"Would you be kind enough to tell Mr. Carrington that I am at home?"

She thought Mr. Curtis seemed surprised that she should know Harry Carrington, but he merely replied:

"I am expecting him this evening and I will give him your message, Miss Braintree."

* * *

Larentia found herself a hackney-carriage, picked up her trunk from number twenty-nine and told the cabman to take her to her home in Lambeth.

As she drove away she found herself thinking how ironic it was that after all the trouble Mr. Carrington had gone to in working out a way in which to obtain the money to save Katie King's life, it was her father who had survived while she had died.

The horror and disgust the Marchioness had felt at the news that her brother had married a Gaiety Girl was now unnecessary and the only people who could be deeply grateful for the whole deception were her father and herself.

'Papa was able to have his operation just because my hair was the same colour as Katie King's,' Larentia thought.

Then she thought it was fate. Perhaps Mr. Curtis was right and he was too important to die.

The hackney-carriage reached Lambeth and the tall house in Wellington Road.

Larentia opened the front door with her key, the cabman set her trunk down in the small hall and she paid his fare, thinking that it came to a lot of money.

When the cabman had driven away and she shut the door behind her, she looked around her with a feeling of dismay and loneliness.

There seemed to be a great deal of dust everywhere and the house seemed very small after the Castle.

She felt now as if her visit there had all been a dream. How could she have stayed in a place that might have been Camelot; met a Knight who might have sat at the Round Table; found him and lost him, and saved her father's life at the expense of breaking her heart?

Then because she felt that all her dreams lay in ruins about her feet, she sat down and cried...

* * *

Harry Carrington arrived when it was dark.

She had been expecting him and had brushed and dusted the Hall and the Sitting-Room, and changed her gown.

She had not eaten anything for the simple reason that she knew her father would not wish her to go shopping so late in the day, and after the luncheon on the train she was not really hungry.

In fact, after crying and feeling a dark depression encompass her whenever she thought of the Duke, she had no wish to do anything but go to bed.

However, she had felt in her bones, as she heard old people say, that when Harry Carrington got her message, he would come to collect the money. Sure enough when it was after nine o'clock, she heard the 'rat-tat' of the knocker.

As he came into the house she saw by the expression on his face, how deeply upset he was by Katie's death.

"I am sorry," she said, before he could speak.

He did not answer for a moment but went into the Sitting-Room, and when she followed him he said savagely:

"Why did she have to die? She was young! She had a lot of life in front of her and quite an enjoyable one too if it brought her what we expected."

Larentia who had been thinking of him rather than herself, felt uncomfortable and she held out the envelope.

"I am afraid there is only £800 in this," she said. "The Duke wanted to make investigations before he gave me any more."

Harry did not speak for a moment, then he said:

"Well, I suppose we should be thankful for small mercies, and now since we cannot stand up to any investigation the chapter is closed."

He opened the envelope, then as he drew the cheque out of it he said:

"How much did you say the Duke had given you?"

"Eight hundred pounds."

"This is made out for a thousand!"

Larentia's eyes widened.

"A thousand?"

"See for yourself."

The Duke's hand-writing was just as she might have expected, strong, upright and forceful, and she knew he had been thinking of her when he had made the cheque out for £200 more than she had asked for, to pay her debts.

"Well, £200 is better than nothing," Harry said with a note of satisfaction in his voice.

He looked at Larentia, then said:

"I suppose now Katie's dead you'll expect half of it?"

"No..no!" Larentia cried. "I do not want..anything. You can keep it all!"

Even as she spoke, she knew she was being stupid, for her father would need nourishing food when he came home, which she had no chance of giving him unless she accepted Harry's offer.

He looked down at the cheque and said:

"There's £200 quid extra here, and from all Dr. Medwin tells me, you're as hard up as I am, so I tell you what we'll do."

Larentia looked at him but she did not speak.

"I'll keep a hundred," he said. "We'll give Katie a decent Funeral instead of letting her be buried on the Parish, and you can have the rest for your father."

Larentia did not speak and he said:

"Come on! Pride's all very well when you can afford it. I peeped in the room after your father had his operation and it's going to be a long time before he is earning any-thing again."

"You are .. right," Larentia said in a small voice. "It is only that . . ."

"The trouble with both of us," Harry interrupted, "is that we are too well-bred to cheat and pretend when we would much rather play it straight. But when you are on the bottom there's nothing you can do but try and kick your way to the top."

"I feel .. ashamed of .. taking the money."

"Of course you do," Harry agreed. "You are too decent for this sort of thing. But have you asked yourself what you would have done if your father had died? You may have a lot of rich relations round the corner, but it doesn't appear they are anxious to be very helpful."

He looked around the small Sitting-Room as he spoke, and as if she saw it for the first time in contrast to the Castle, Larentia knew how poverty-stricken it appeared.

"Things will improve when Papa can start writing again," she said defensively.

"I hope so, but his books, although they are brilliant, do not sell. Medwin told me all about them."

"Then I shall accept your .. offer, and spend every penny of it on Papa."

She spoke almost passionately and it made Harry look at her in surprise. Then his eyes narrowed.

"What happened when you were at the Castle?"

"H . happened?"

"What has upset you personally, apart from having to lie and pretend to be Katie?"

"N . nothing."

"Now you *are* lying," he said, then exclaimed : "I know what has occurred. You have fallen in love with the Duke! I suppose he was there. When I was reading the newspaper-cuttings about the Marchioness I saw pictures of him."

There was no need for Larentia to answer.

The colour that flooded into her face and the manner

in which she turned away told Harry the truth.

After a moment he asked:

"What are you going to do about it?"

"Nothing .. and I can get no more .. money for you."

"You don't intend to see him again?"

"No, no! Never!"

The words burst from her lips without her meaning to say them.

Harry put the cheque in his pocket.

"If Katie had been alive," he said quietly, "she would know you did an excellent job on her behalf and were a real sport about it, and that's exactly what you have been. I am grateful, although I don't suppose you will ever tell your father what happened. But he will be grateful because he is alive."

"It was .. you who .. saved him."

She turned round again.

"I shall always thank you," she said, "it is just that .. I feel .. embarrassed at having taken so much .. money under false pretences, and I wish we could afford to .. send back the two hundred pounds."

"I have to save you from your better nature," Harry said with a smile. "No, Larentia, 'let sleeping dogs lie', and when the Duke realises as doubtless he will, sooner or later, if he tries to look for you, that Katie is dead, then the whole episode will be forgotten."

"How will he learn that?" Larentia asked.

Harry shrugged his shoulders.

"I presume it depends how much he wants to see you again and to tell you what he has discovered in his investigations. After all, I presume he really believes you are the Duchess of Tregaron?"

"Yes .. I think he .. believed I was .. but the Marchioness was very hostile and very .. shocked at the idea."

"Well, she'll be glad Katie's dead!"

There was a note in his voice that told Larentia how much it meant to him.

"I am sorry for your sake," she said softly.

"I loved her!" Harry replied. "God knows why! There've been a lot of women in my life, one way or another, but Katie meant more to me than any of the others. And although we were too poor for comfort, it didn't matter all that amount. We used to laugh and joke about it and she always said: 'There's better times just round the corner'."

"I .. I am so .. sorry," Larentia said again.

"Perhaps in a month or so I'll find it easier to forget," Harry said. "And the hundred quid you brought me will help a great deal."

"You will .. pay Mr. Levy?" Larentia asked quickly.

"Yes, of course," he answered, "and that reminds me, you had better endorse this cheque, it's made out to Miss Katie King. Or, if you like, I will do it for you."

"You .. do it."

She had a feeling she could not lie any more about something which had belonged to the Duke.

"All right," Harry said. "I'll come and see you tomorrow and tell you what time the Funeral is. You'll come, won't you? There's not likely to be many people there. As far as I know, Katie had no relatives, and not many friends, except me."

"Yes .. of course I will come."

"She'll have a decent coffin, and I'll get her some flowers," Harry said. "She'd like that."

He went towards the front door and Larentia followed him.

As she opened it, it struck him that she looked very forlorn and somehow frail and insubstantial, in the flickering light of two candles.

"You'll be all right alone?" he asked.

"Quite all right," she answered.

"Well, bolt the door after I've gone, and don't open it unless you know who is outside."

"No .. of course not."

"You ought to have someone with you," he said, almost to himself.

He hesitated for a moment as if he had a suggestion to make, but decided against it and without saying any more, he left.

Larentia shut the door and bolted it. Then she began to blow out the candles, preparatory to going to bed.

Chapter Seven

Larentia came down the stairs wearing the black gown she had worn when her mother died.

It was a little tight for her and in consequence made her look slimmer and more elegant than usual.

Her small bonnet was trimmed with black ribbons and she had a pair of black gloves.

All the time she was dressing she had tried to think of Katie and how tragic it was that she should die when she was so young.

But irresistibly her mind was back at the Castle and all she could see when she looked in the mirror was not herself but the huge stone walls with their arrow-slit windows and castellated towers.

For the two days she had been alone at home, not speaking to anyone except when she visited her father in the Nursing Home, she had been haunted by the Duke.

She knew that having once found the most precious possession in the world – the Holy Grail of Love – she had lost it and would never find it again.

To her the Castle was Camelot and the Duke in her dreams was as she had seen him first in 'silver-shining armour starry clear. She knew that never again could a man mean anything to her and she no longer had a heart to give because it was for ever his.

"I love you! I love you!" she whispered at night into her pillow and felt she was past crying, for her whole body was one aching longing for the touch of his lips.

She told herself now that she must come back to the real world and keep her memories of the Duke for times when she was reading her father's books or losing herself in the vivid descriptions of King Arthur and his Knights in Tennyson's poems.

There was a knock at the door and she knew it would be Harry Carrington come to collect her as he had promised to do to take her to Katie's Funeral.

She let him in and saw that he had a hackney-carriage outside. But first he walked into the small Sitting-Room and took an envelope from his pocket.

"Here's your share," he said. "£75!"

He put the envelope down on her father's desk, and Larentia parted her lips to say she had changed her mind and she would not take it.

Then she remembered that her father was still weak, and even though Mr. Curtis had said he might be able to come home in another ten days, it would be months before he was able to walk again, and during that time he must eat nourishing food and not be worried by financial difficulties.

"Thank..you," Larentia said in a low voice.

"The Funeral cost just over £20," Harry said, "and the rest I've spent on flowers."

He spoke with an almost defiant note in his voice as if he expected her to find fault. When Larentia said nothing, he turned towards the door and she knew by the expression on his face that he was suffering.

She was just about to follow him when she said :

"One moment. I wanted to ask you whether we should somehow let the Duke know that Miss King..is dead..."

Her voice faltered for a moment, then she went on :

"It seems..wrong that we should let them continue to ..worry about the..money I asked for when there is no longer any..reason for them to..pay it."

"They'll doubtless be glad about that!" Harry replied sharply, "but even more glad to know they need not have a Duchess who would, in their eyes, disgrace their quarterings."

"The Duke did say," Larentia murmured, "that she should be .. included on their genealogical tree."

To her surprise Harry laughed and it was not a very pleasant sound, before he said :

"That's the sort of thing he would think of! Well, he need not trouble himself. I expect sooner or later he'll find out the truth and realise he's been had for a mug even if it was only to the tune of a thousand pounds!"

As he stopped speaking he realised that Larentia was staring at him with a horrified expression on her face.

"Wh . what are you .. saying?" she asked in a faltering voice. "Are you .. telling me that what I .. told the Duke was .. untrue and Miss King was not .. married to his uncle?"

"Of course she wasn't married," Harry replied. "Do you really think the almighty, stuck-up Duke of Tregaron would take a chorus-girl for a wife?"

"B . but the .. letter and the .. Marriage Certificate," Larentia gasped.

"Very skilfully executed by one of the best forgers in the business! And I pride myself that the finishing touch was the entry in the Marriage Register at Southwark Cathedral."

He paused before he added :

"My plan deceived you and it apparently deceived the Duke. I hope he goes on sweating over it just as all those stuck-up aristocrats deserve for their attitude of — 'I'm holier than thou!'"

"B . but how could you .. how could you let me tell such lies? And receive money for them?" Larentia asked.

There was a sob in her voice and Harry said savagely :

"Have you forgotten that I invented them to save Katie's life and you told them to save your father's? Well, I failed, but you should be thankful things turned out as they did."

Larentia shut her eyes for a moment as if she fought for self-control. Then she said very quietly :

"You are right .. I should be .. grateful. Let us .. go."

She did not wait for Harry but walked ahead of him, opened the front door leaving him to close it behind them, and stepped into the hackney-carriage.

It was not far to the Churchyard but she had the feeling that Harry had taken a carriage because it showed more respect for Katie than if they arrived on foot.

They drove in silence. Larentia was very pale and she felt that in learning the truth it was as if Harry had hit her over the head with a club.

How could she have known .. how could she have guessed for one moment that he was .. lying, that the documents she carried were forgeries, and that Katie had, in fact, been everything the Garons had suspected her of being?

As the Churchyard came into view Harry said:

"Stop worrying, Larentia, about your part in this affair. No-one could ever blame you for acting in good faith in trying to save two people's lives."

He looked at her pale cheeks and down-cast eyes and added:

"Forget the Duke. He can mean nothing in your life, and at least he has not violated you as his uncle did Katie."

"I will .. try to forget .. him."

"That's sensible," Harry approved. "We've both got something to forget and the sooner we do so the better for both of us."

The horses came to a standstill and Harry stepped out of the carriage, paid the cabman and he and Larentia walked up the path towards the Church.

Katie's coffin stood at the bottom of the Chancel steps. There were two large wreaths on it which Larentia knew must be the ones which she had paid for.

There were also a few bunches of flowers and from where she was sitting, she could see that one of them had been sent by the girls of the Gaiety Theatre.

There were only four other people in the Church besides themselves: an elderly woman who looked like a theatrical dresser, a man who appeared to have something of the Theatre about him, two girls with painted faces who Larentia guessed were from the Gaiety and was sure of it when they smiled and nodded at Harry.

She knelt down in one of the pews on the opposite side of the aisle and prayed that Katie would find peace and happiness wherever she might be.

Then because she could not help herself she prayed that the Duke would forgive her for deceiving him and that in the future he might remember their love.

Not with contempt but as something very beautiful and mystical which had passed through their lives, and brought them a beauty which could never be despoiled.

The Parson came in with a hurried air as if he was aware he was late and was trying to make up for it.

His surplice was creased and needed washing and he repeated the Funeral Service without giving the words any particular meaning or even sounding very sincere.

Then the pall-bearers lifted the coffin onto their shoulders and Larentia and Harry walked immediately behind them while the other people followed.

Katie was to be buried in a far corner of the Churchyard, and they picked their way amongst ancient graves, many of the head-stones being broken or crooked.

The grass was over-grown and Larentia thought that the whole Churchyard had an air of neglect as if no-one was interested in it.

Then she told herself she must not think of anything but Katie and when they reached the grave-side she tried to remember that it was only Katie's body they were committing into the ground but her spirit was free and she was no longer in pain.

She shut her eyes and prayed:

"Oh, God, let her be happy with you and let her forget everything she has suffered here on earth."

Then as if she could not help herself the prayer in her heart turned to one for herself.

"And help me to forget .. please God .. help me to learn to live without him .. so that the pain that I feel now will lessen .. and I shall only be grateful for having once known the love that is part of You..."

The coffin was being lowered slowly into the ground and she opened her eyes.

On the other side of the grave she saw a man standing and as she looked at him, she thought with a sudden constriction of her heart, that she must be dreaming.

It was the Duke.

* * *

The Duke was in his Study when his Comptroller Mr. Arran came into the room.

"Jackson is here, Your Grace."

The Duke rose from his desk.

"Show him in, Arran," he said. "I want to hear why he has been so long."

"I am sure he has a reasonable explanation to give Your Grace," Mr. Arran replied, with just a note of rebuke in his voice.

He was, in fact, extremely grateful that the detective he had employed on the Duke's orders had at last answered his summons to come to Tregaron House as soon as he had anything to report.

Ever since the Duke had arrived in London he had enquired a dozen times a day as to whether the detective had any news for him, and he was obviously extremely annoyed when the reply was not what he desired.

In fact, Mr. Arran was finding it very difficult to understand why the Duke was in such an obvious state of agitation over a Gaiety Girl who purported to have been married secretly to the late Duke.

He had known the 4th Duke and worked for him for over fifteen years, and he did not believe for a moment that he would, however ardently he desired a son, have married one of the women he desired for a very different reason.

Debauched, depraved and taking for his companions

144

some of the most vile creatures in London, he had nevertheless always been extremely conscious of his own importance and, in his own way, proud of his family history.

In fact Mr. Arran was astonished that the new Duke believed for a moment that the tale of a marriage, even with the evidence of a Certificate was true. He was almost sure that the letter, although it certainly appeared to be in the Duke's handwriting, was a forgery.

He was well aware, however, that to substantiate his convictions they needed proof, and he had been waiting for the detective and his findings almost as eagerly as the Duke had.

Now with an undoubted note of triumph in his voice he announced:

"Mr. Jackson, Your Grace!"

The detective walked into the room.

He was small, a rather ferrety-looking man and, the Duke thought, exactly what he might have expected a detective to look like.

"Good-morning, Your Grace."

"Good-morning," the Duke replied, "I hope, Mr. Jackson, you have something to tell me. I have been waiting for your report ever since I arrived in London.'

"I know that, Your Grace, but it's not been at all easy to get the information you required."

"But you have it now?"

"Yes, Your Grace."

The Duke, with an expression of relief on his face, sat down at his desk and indicated a chair at the side of it.

The detective seated himself and drew from his pocket a number of carefully written notes.

"On Mr. Arran's instructions, Your Grace," he began, "I went to the Gaiety Theatre and ascertained that Miss Katie King had performed in all the Shows put on by Mr. Hollingshead over the last six years."

He paused to note that the Duke was listening intently, and continued:

"Before that she appeared at the Olympia Music Hall and had come to London when she was just seventeen, from Stockport."

"I know all this," the Duke said.

"I'm glad that what I've discovered confirms what Your Grace has been told."

Mr. Jackson turned over a page and went on :

"Miss King had a small part in every Show which became a popular item with the audience in that her hair, which I understand was a very attractive colour, fell down during her dance. They waited for it to happen and applauded when it did."

"Go on," the Duke urged. "I want to know where she is now."

"I'm coming to that, Your Grace. In the last year Miss King has moved several times from one lodging to another, but lately she had a room in Lambeth."

"What is the address?"

"Quay Street, Your Grace, Number ninety-two, but it's not, if I may say so, a particularly salubrious neighbourhood."

"She is there now?"

"No, Your Grace. Apparently some six to seven weeks ago Miss King left the Gaiety. She was not well."

The Duke moved a little restlessly as if he was aware of this.

"She stayed at home at ninety-two Quay Street with a man who has been with her for the last four years."

"Man? What man?"

Mr. Jackson turned over a page of his notebook.

"His name's Harry Carrington, Your Grace, and he's well known in the Theatre World as a 'hanger on' of actresses or dancers who are making a fair amount of money from their 'profession'."

The way Mr. Jackson spoke insinuated a number of extensions of the word 'profession'.

"Apparently," he continued, "Harry Carrington had

been unusually faithful in staying with Katie King for far longer than is expected in such liaisons."

To his surprise the Duke rose from the chair in which he was sitting to move to the window to stand staring out.

Still he did not speak, and after a moment of indecision Mr. Jackson went on :

"I learned from the other people in the house that a doctor came frequently to visit Miss King. Then at the beginning of last week she went away."

He paused but there was no response from the Duke and he said, with a touch of pride in his voice :

"It wasn't easy for me to discover where she had gone, but eventually I followed Harry Carrington who continued to sleep in the room they had shared in Quay Street. He led me to a house in Harley Street."

"Harley Street?" the Duke said sharply. "What number?"

"49, Your Grace. It's the house and Nursing Home that belongs to a well-known Surgeon by the name of Sheldon Curtis."

"And she is there now?"

"No, Your Grace. Miss King died three days ago!"

Mr. Jackson spoke again with that little note of triumph at his own cleverness and also with an awareness of the almost sensational finale to his tale.

To his surprise he saw that the Duke was glaring at him as if he could not believe what he had heard. Then he said in a voice that was aggressively hoarse :

"Did you say Miss King had – died?"

"Yes, Your Grace."

"I do not believe you!"

"But it's true, Your Grace, and she is, in fact, being buried this morning. There's no doubt about that. Mr. Curtis told me so himself."

The Duke turned to stare once again out of the window.

Mr. Jackson waited, thinking the silence was very oppressive, until the Duke asked :

"Where is she being buried?"

"In the Churchyard of the Parish Church of Lambeth, Your Grace. St. Mary's. I think the Funeral's at noon."

Again there was silence. Then, without speaking, without even looking at the detective, the Duke walked swiftly from the room.

*　　*　　*

The grave-diggers were shovelling earth onto the coffin and Larentia could only stand feeling as if the Duke's eyes on the other side of the grave held her captive, and it was impossible for her to move or even breathe.

The Parson said the last words of the Service and as he turned to walk back towards the Church the girls from the Gaiety moved to Harry's side to start talking to him.

Larentia did not even hear them.

She was conscious of nothing but the Duke and she knew as he walked round the grave to her side, that her will had gone and she only knew that inevitably fate had caught up with her and there was no appeal against it.

Without speaking he put his hand over her arm and drew her away from the grave and back past the broken tombstones down the path to the lychgate to where his carriage was waiting outside.

He helped her into it and only as the footman placed a rug over their knees did he ask:

"Where do you live?"

For a moment it was impossible for her to reply. Then in a voice that trembled Larentia answered:

"20 Wellington..Road..it is the house on the.. corner."

The footman shut the door and a moment later the carriage drove off.

Larentia's heart was beating tumultuously and her voice seemed to have died in her throat. It was impossible for her even to look at the Duke or wonder what he was thinking.

She clasped her fingers in her black gloves together to

148

stare straight ahead, thinking only that he was there, he was beside her and it was a wonder beyond words, even though he knew that she was a liar and a cheat.

'I cannot even give him his money back,' she thought despairingly, and wondered if he would understand when she told him why she had needed it.

The carriage came to a standstill outside her home and still feeling as if her will-power had gone and she was a puppet with the Duke pulling the strings, Larentia stepped out and fumbled in her bag for the key.

The Duke took it from her and opened the door.

As they went into the small Hall and across it into the Sitting-Room Larentia wondered what he must think of her surroundings after having seen her against the background of the Castle and the beauty of it which would always be to her the mysticism of Camelot.

As she reached the centre of the room she turned to face him.

Then as her eyes met his, the spell that had held them silent was broken and the words came tumbling to her lips.

"F..forgive me..please..forgive me," she pleaded. "I did not..mean to deceive you in the..way I..did. I.. s.swear to you I did not know that..Katie King was not married..to your uncle as I was..told she was."

She drew in her breath before she went on:

"I..needed the m.money desperately to save both my father and Miss King from dying of..c.cancer..but I believed she really had been..married secretly to the D. Duke, and it seemed at the time that nothing..mattered except that she and..my father should live ..."

Tears had come to her eyes as she spoke, and it was diffi-cult to see the expression on the Duke's face, but she felt it must be one of condemnation.

Then he asked quietly:

"What is your name?"

"Larentia Braintree..my..my father writes..books on

Mediaeval History, especially the Arthurian legends..
which is why I know so much about them."

"Are you telling me that your father is Professor
Braintree who wrote *The Truth About King Arthur* and
translated the Welsh poem : *Y Gododdin* ?"

"Yes .. You have .. heard of him ?"

"Of course I have heard of him !" the Duke replied. "I
have every book he has ever written in the Library at the
Castle, if you had asked to see them."

Larentia drew in her breath.

"Perhaps then you will .. understand why I .. behaved as
I did," she said. "Papa was .. dying and the doctor said the
only chance there was of .. saving him was if he could be
operated on by Mr. Sheldon Curtis, and it would cost .. two
hundred pounds !"

She made a helpless little gesture with her hands.

"It was .. impossible to find so much money .. and when
Mr. Carrington . . . "

"What is that man to you?" the Duke interrupted
sharply.

"Katie King was attended by the same doctor who
looked after Papa. Mr. Carrington came to see me with the
suggestion that because she had been married to your uncle
we could obtain .. money for both her and Papa to be ..
operated on by Mr. Sheldon Curtis."

"That meant you needed £400," the Duke said. "Why
did you insist on £800?"

"The money had to be .. borrowed from a Usurer called
.. Isaac Levy and he demanded .. 100% interest !"

Somehow Larentia thought this made her whole behaviour seem even more degrading than it was already.

"I am .. sorry," she said again.

Now she could not prevent the tears from over-flowing
from her eyes and running down her cheeks.

"So the operations took place while you were at the
Castle," the Duke said, as if he was reasoning it out for
himself, "but Katie King died."

"Mr. Curtis said she was in a much worse..condition than..Papa."

"Your father will recover?"

"Completely! He is coming..home in ten days."

"In the meantime you are living here alone?"

"I..I am..all right."

"Have you thought about the Castle since you ran away from me?"

"Y.yes..of course I have."

It was difficult to say the words and she knew he was waiting for an answer.

"Is that all?"

"A..all?"

"Have you not thought about me?"

She felt him come nearer to her as he spoke, and now because there was a note in his voice that had been there the night he had kissed her, she said a little incoherently:

"Forgive..me..please..forgive me. I know what I did ..was..wicked..but..Papa is alive..and perhaps you can..understand how much that..matters."

"That is not what I asked you," the Duke insisted.

She felt herself tremble because his voice seemed to vibrate through her and she said quickly:

"I have..thought about you..of course I have..and I felt perhaps you would be..angry when I disappeared .I did not..mean you ever to see me again..so..there was.. nothing else I could do."

"Why not?"

Now there was a silence that seemed to Larentia to be full of meaning.

She did not want to answer, but knew the Duke was waiting and in a voice he could hardly hear, she whispered:

"Because..I could not..do what you..asked...It would have been..wrong and would have..spoilt our.. love."

"Our love?" he enquired. "So you did love me!"

"Of course I..loved you!" she replied a little wildly.

"I loved you from the first moment when I thought you came to me in..silver shining armour..and when you kissed me..I knew that I had seen and touched..the Holy Grail."

Her voice died away. Then she whispered:

"But I could not..allow you to..soil what was.. sacred and part of God..or allow you to be..part of what..would be a..sin."

"So you were thinking of me!"

"I shall always think of you," Larentia said, "but you belong to Camelot..and you must go back there and do everything that is..fine, noble and great..because that is what is..expected of you."

She paused, then said, as if she could not help herself:

"But please..think of me..just sometimes..when you are..alone."

"Do you really think that would be enough?" the Duke asked. "Do you believe I could be content with only thoughts of you, Larentia?"

"There is.. nothing else I can..give you," she whispered and her voice broke on the words.

She thought the Duke would turn and leave her. But when it was an agony to stand with tears running down her face waiting to hear him go, he put his hands on her shoulders and turned her round to face him.

She made a little murmur of protest, then instinctively she looked up into his eyes and was lost.

All she could see was the expression in them and his face which had always to her been the embodiment of everything that was fine and noble in the legends of the Knights of the Round Table.

She felt the Duke's fingers through the thin material of her gown and she was aware of the closeness of him and how strong and overpowering he was.

Then he asked, and she thought there was a hint of laughter in his voice:

"Are you really trying to send me away, Larentia? How

could you do such a thing when you know that neither of us could be complete without the other?"

"You have to .. go," she replied. "There is .. nothing else we .. can do .. and I have tried to make you .. understand."

"I do understand," the Duke said, "but I am not asking you, my precious, to do anything that is secret or wrong. I was crazy to think that was possible in the first place. I am asking you if you will marry me, and together we will make the Castle the Camelot it was always meant to be."

For a moment Larentia felt as if she could not have heard him aright, and must have dreamt what he was saying.

Then as she looked at him, her eyes shining through her tears and her lips trembling because she was both afraid and excited at the same time, he pulled her against him and his mouth came down on hers.

It was so wonderful, so rapturous after her belief that she had lost him and would never know such ecstasy again, that she wished for a moment that she could die.

Then as his kiss became more demanding, more insistent, she wanted to live.

The wonder he had evoked in her before swept over them both, and Larentia felt as if once again he carried her up to the very throne of God, and they were neither of them human, but divine...

Only very much later, it might have been a few minutes or a century of time, the Duke raised his head and she said incoherently:

"I .. I love you .. did you really say that I could .. stay with you and .. love you .. or did I dream it?"

"We are both dreaming," the Duke answered in his deep voice. "I have thought and dreamt of you since I first saw your picture and now I can hardly believe that the goddess I have worshipped all my life is here in my arms."

He drew her beside him and kissed her again fiercely and demandingly then said with what sounded like a note of anger in his voice:

"How could you leave me? How could you go away in that cruel manner? You have driven me nearly crazy these past few days and when I was told you were dead, the world came to an end!"

"I .. I am .. sorry," Larentia said again. "Please .. please forgive me .. and show me how I can make it up to you."

"You can only do that by loving me."

"I do love you .. I love you until it has been an .. agony for me to be alone in this house .. with only thoughts of you to haunt me."

"That is something that will never happen again," the Duke said. "I will look after you, protect you, and never, my darling, leave you alone. You are far too beautiful for one thing."

He untied the ribbons of her small bonnet as he spoke and threw it on the floor, then his hand was on her hair, touching the soft silkiness of it, seeing the little flicker of fire amongst the gold glinting in the sunshine coming in through the window.

"I want to see you with your hair falling over your shoulders," he said. "Tell me, my precious, how soon will you marry me?"

"What will .. the Marchioness .. say?"

"What everybody else will say when they know you — that I am the luckiest man in the whole world!" the Duke replied. "And anyway, does it matter to you or me what anyone says? You are mine, Larentia, and no-one with any brains could help admiring the brilliance of your father."

Larentia gave a little cry of sheer happiness.

"If only Papa could hear you say that."

"When can I see him?"

"He is not allowed any visitors for the moment, except for me, but .. perhaps you will be the .. exception."

"As his son-in-law I shall be entitled to the privilege," the Duke said. "But you still have not answered my question. When will you marry me?"

"When do you .. want me?"

"Now! At this moment! I will get a Special Licence and we can be married tomorrow."

Larentia moved a little closer to him.

"Are you sure..quite sure this is..something you..should do?"

He turned her face up to his.

"It is something I intend to do," he said. "You know, my sweet darling, that you belong to the Castle as I do. It is part of us both, and just as the legends of King Arthur are real to you, so they are to me. Somehow, although I cannot explain it, we are part of them and still living with them."

"And it is true..completely and absolutely true," Larentia cried, "but I never thought I would ever find anyone who understood. I love you..and I will try to do everything that is..right and good so that you need never be ashamed of me..and I swear that..never again will I ever..lie to you."

"I know that," he said gently. "And, my adorable darling, we are both so incredibly, unbelievably fortunate to have found each other."

There was a note of reverence in his voice that made Larentia feel almost as if she heard the wings of angels moving around them. Then she whispered:

"I will grow 'one with you and believe as you believe'."

"You are already 'one with me'," he replied. "You are mine! Your heart and your soul are mine, and tomorrow we will be one with our bodies and therefore complete. A man and a woman, my darling, as God intended us to be, except that you are my goddess and I am very content to worship at your shrine."

"You must not..say such..things."

Then as his lips held her captive Larentia knew they were one as he had said they were; inseparable for all time, and also one with all the mystery and magic of the legends to which they both belonged.

The love which had come to them was the perfect manifestation of God's divine gift to mankind that he should seek in his heart and soul for the Holy Grail as King Arthur's Knights had done.

It was a love that could only be expressed by the 'silver-shining armour starry clear' which vibrates from God to man.

Other books by Barbara Cartland

Romantic novels, over 250, the most recently published being:
Bride to the King
Only Love
The Dawn of Love
Love Has His Way
The Explosion of Love
Women Have Hearts
A Gentleman in Love
A Heart is Stolen
The Power and the Prince
Free From Fear
A Song of Love
Love for Sale
Little White Doves of Love
The Perfection of Love
Lost Laughter
Punished with Love
Lucifer and the Angel
Love at the Helm
Ola and the Sea Wolf
The Prude and the Prodigal

Autobiographical and Biographical
The Isthmus Years 1919–1939
The Years of Opportunity 1939–1945
I Search for Rainbows 1945–1976
We Danced All Night 1919–1929
Ronald Cartland (with a foreword by Sir Winston Churchill)
Polly My Wonderful Mother
I Seek the Miraculous

Historical
Bewitching Women
The Outrageous Queen (The Story of Queen Christina of Sweden)
The Scandalous Life of King Carol
The Private Life of King Charles II
The Private Life of Elizabeth, Empress of Austria
Josephine, Empress of France
Diane de Poitiers
Metternich – the Passionate Diplomat

Sociology
You in the Home
The Fascinating Forties
Marriage for Moderns
Be Vivid, Be Vital
Love, Life and Sex
Vitamins for Vitality
Husbands and Wives
Etiquette
The Many Facets of Love
Sex and the Teenager
The Book of Charm
Living Together
The Youth Secret
The Magic of Honey
Barbara Cartland's Book of Beauty and Health
Men are Wonderful

Cookery
Barbara Cartland's Health Food Cookery Book
Food for Love
Magic of Honey Cookbook
Recipes for Lovers

Editor of
The Common Problems by Ronald Cartland
(with a preface by the Rt. Hon. the Earl of Selborne, P.C.)
Barbara Cartland's Library of Love
Barbara Cartland's Library of Ancient Wisdom

Drama
Blood Money
French Dressing

Philosophy
Touch the Stars

Radio operetta
The Rose and the Violet (Music by Mark Lubbock)
performed in 1942

Radio plays
The Caged Bird: An episode in the Life of Elizabeth
Empress of Austria. Performed in 1957

General
Barbara Cartland's Book of Celebrities
Barbara Cartland's Book of Useless Information (Foreword by
The Earl Mountbatten of Burma)
Love and Lovers (picture book)
The Light of Love (prayer book)

Verse
Lines on Life and Love

Music
An Album of Love Songs sung with the Royal Philharmonic Orchestra

Magazine
Barbara Cartland's World of Romance

Barbara Cartland
The Prude and the Prodigal 80p

The new Earl had the raffish look of a pirate or buccaneer and seemed
intent on selling the treasures of Winslow Hall to pay for his
amusements. Prunella thought him an unlikely means of saving her
sister from the attentions of his nephew, a dandy and fortune-hunter.
Only after verbal duels, misunderstandings, and a fateful theatre visit
were Prunella's problems solved and the tables turned, as the Duke's
demanding kisses taught her of love's irresistibility.

A Song of Love 75p

Because of Lady Sherington's urgent need for money, Trina had planned
to aid the elderly Marchioness of Clevedon in her search for truth, while
passing herself and her mother off as twins. Would the Marchioness's
perceptive son wreck her schemes? Would the fairytale castle in
Provence yield up its secrets? And could Trina and the Marquis revel in
a tempestuous passion?

You can buy these and other Barbara Cartland books from booksellers and
newsagents; or direct from the following address:
Pan Books, Sales Office, Cavaye Place, London SW10 9PG
Send purchase price plus 20p for the first book and 10p for
each additional book to allow for postage and packing
Prices quoted are applicable in the UK

While every effort is made to keep prices low, it is sometimes
necessary to increase prices at short notice. Pan Books reserve
the right to show on covers and charge new retail prices which
may differ from those advertised in the text or elsewhere